Baby For The Billionaire

Erica Frost

Published by Erica Frost, 2023.

This is a work of fiction. Similarities to real people, places, or events are entirely coincidental.

BABY FOR THE BILLIONAIRE

First edition. June 24, 2023.

Copyright © 2023 Erica Frost.

ISBN: 979-8223279068

Written by Erica Frost.

Table of Contents

Baby For The Billionaire
New Adult Second Chance Romance

By: Erica Frost

Foreword

Have you ever had your heart broken – really broken? It never heals, not properly. It took me a long time to pick myself up, finish college and put my life back on track. I got a job, found a boyfriend and then, I saw him again. My new boss was the same guy who dumped me in college. That same arrogant, selfish bastard. I never wanted to see it then, but I was older now. Wiser. I would not make the same mistake again. But he was older too, sexier, and richer. More into me than before and when I pushed him away, he made my life a living hell. The last thing I thought would ever happen, somehow, did. When I found out I was pregnant, I knew that I had to find a way to win this game – for once and for all.

Baby For The Billionaire

Chapter 1

Lauren

That morning, I had a feeling something was about to happen.

Standing in my underwear, about to get dressed, my hand hesitated before I took out the top I'd been planning to wear today. It seemed wrong, somehow. I bit my lip as I looked for my jeans, then stepped back, pausing.

Not jeans.

Not today.

It was the end of the week, and I didn't have that many clean clothes left. There wasn't time to think about it too much, I never had much time in the morning, certainly not to plan a whole new outfit. I usually thought about what I would wear the following day as I went to bed, to ensure I didn't waste time in the morning.

But the voice in my head was urging me to wear something nice, something different. Sexy. I couldn't think why. It was Friday after all and there was a drinks thing at the new office, after work. But these were informal events, I probably would go for a few drinks with my team and come home. It wasn't like I was wanting to meet anyone or had my eye on someone either, I was happy with Dax, my boyfriend of the past three months. Things were going well, and I was happy with him.

Happy enough.

And, yet.

I glanced at the time and looked through the clothes in my wardrobe, finally settling on a short skirt and tights, with a little top that I always got complimented on. I slipped on a denim jacket over that and looked in the mirror. Yup. That would work.

There was only time for a few gulps of coffee and a slice of dry toast as I rushed to get to work. The apartment was quiet. My mother wasn't up yet, but the school where she taught art was nearby. She could afford to get up a whole hour later than I did.

It was my first week in the new job and I couldn't afford to make a bad impression. I had struggled for months to find something suitable and this job as Community Manager for Egal was an absolute dream come true. I ran social media in the communications department. There was plenty of opportunity to move up, to move to another branch anywhere in the country, even overseas. Egal was a global company of consumer goods, owning several brands and getting in had not been easy. There had been several rounds of interviews and fortunately, someone on the interviewing panel liked my Instagram account and I was hired.

"Don't you look nice?!" Petra smiled at me as I arrived on our floor. I greeted her and made my way to my desk in the corner. There were two others seated close by, Jane, who did our press releases and general media and Tash, who focused more on internal communications. All of us reported to Diaz, the Head of Communications. I spent the day checking various accounts and feeds to see if anything had been reported about the company, looked out for trends, and came up with a few ideas for company campaigns. Five minutes to five, Tash winked at me, "Let's get ready!"

"Isn't it too soon?" I looked around nervously, I didn't want anyone seeing us skipping work early to go drinking.

"Are you kidding? Most of the office has already left! I'm going to put on some make-up," she said and left for the bathroom. I looked around and saw that Diaz was getting ready to leave too, grabbing his jacket.

"You girls coming?" he asked, looking at me. "End of your first week, right? You did good; congratulations! Come on, the drinks are on me!"

"The drinks are on the company, you mean!" Petra said and Diaz grinned. I was still wary around him, but the company didn't seem to take office hierarchy too seriously. Or maybe he was just a nice guy. As we all walked down to the elevator, I heard that Friday drinks usually happened once a month. There was a bar near the office where everyone gathered. I was looking forward to seeing what the rest of the company looked like. So far, I'd only seen some of the marketing and sales staff in the elevator.

"What do you think, will the new job work out?" Petra teased, as Diaz and Tash walked on ahead to the bar.

"Definitely!" I said, at once. "I've got so many ideas!"

"Good!" she said, tucking her arm through mine and hurrying me along to the bar. When we got there, it was already quite crowded and there was loud music pumping over the speakers. It was almost impossible to have a conversation. We found a space to stand, and Tash pointed out a few people to me. Then we had a round of shooters, then another and I could feel the alcohol going straight to my head. Diaz left some time after that, and Tash and Petra started to drink seriously. When more colleagues left, we found a table and started playing drinking games. Then followed a round of truth or dare. Some other people I didn't even know joined in. Suddenly, they were all looking at me.

"Truth or dare!" someone yelled, and I don't know why, but I said "Dare."

There was clapping and yelling to that, and someone said, "I dare you to grab someone's ass."

"What?"

"You know, like they do to us, a sneaky hand below your butt cheek and give it a good squeeze!"

The girls were hooting with laughter.

I didn't want to get into trouble, it being my first week and all, but Petra assured me we weren't at the office. "Everyone here is relaxed and this is after hours, so I wouldn't worry about it! Come on, pick someone!"

I looked at the crowd and felt my heartbeat quicken as I checked out the men. "You did say it had to be a man, right?"

Tash and Petra laughed out loud, and I felt myself going along with it. They were nudging me with their elbows, pointing out potential candidates.

"What about him, check out the butt on him!"

"Oh yeah, I'll have me some of that!"

There were howling with laughter, and I shook my head, even though I was smiling. They were having a good time, letting their hair down after a long week. I liked them and wanted to be a part of the group. My eye caught someone standing at the bar, with his back to me. He was tall and well-built, wearing designer jeans and a simple, but smart shirt. His stance was casual, but I could tell he was in good shape, that he looked after himself. He had one hand in his pocket, and he seemed to be in conversation with the guy next to him. I liked the shape of his head, and his hair, which was a bit longer, and wavy.

"You found someone?" Tash asked me, giggling.

"Maybe," I smiled.

"Go on, do it!" The rest of the table started egging me on, chanting "do it, do it" but fortunately it was so noisy in the bar that no one else heard. I got up and made my way across to the bar, looking over my shoulder at the girls sitting at the table nodding encouragement at me.

I didn't mind doing it, to be honest. I had always been a good sport and liked getting up to high jinks in college too. I didn't think about it too much, walking up until I was close behind him, then checking that the girls were watching. Then I slid my hand over his backside, cupping one of his butt cheeks and gently caressing it with my hand. I pulled my hand away as I heard the girls explode with laughter. The man turned around to face me.

"That's one way to grab my ...uhm...attention," he said, and I looked up into his face, laughing already as I had my apology ready.

That was when I recognized him.

Oh, my God. I couldn't believe it. It was Matthew, the guy who'd dumped me in college four years ago. I saw recognition flash through his eyes too. The smile was wiped from his face.

"Matthew?"

"Lauren?"

We stared at each other, stunned speechless for a moment.

"I didn't ... didn't know it was you," I finally managed to explain, rather badly. "The girls dared me to do it," I said, pointing to my co-workers who were giggling like teenagers at the table.

"Hi Tash, Petra," he called out to them. They waved back, a bit sheepishly.

"Wait, you know them?"

"They work for me, at Egal?" He turned back to the bar to get his beer.

It took a moment for his words to sink in.

"For you? They work for you?"

Did it mean I worked for him too?

"I'm the CEO of Egal Incorporated. Didn't you know?"

"Then... I'm your new Community Manager," I stammered.

"Really?"

"You didn't know?"

"HR does all of the hiring, usually."

He looked at me for a moment, holding my gaze. I felt a shiver of something down my back. Anticipation? Could it be desire? Matthew had always been so good-looking, so bloody sexy. I had always found him devilishly attractive, and he had aged well, too. But, as I didn't have to remind myself, he had dumped me at the end of his senior year. Broken my heart, to be honest. I had not told anyone, certainly never let him know how badly he'd hurt me. I'd been devastated. Even though I was always trying to play it cool and keep it light between us, I'd fallen for him. Hard. I thought he had felt the same way. The connection between us had been so powerful and intense. But the way it had ended, that had been brutal. I would never forgive him for that.

"I wouldn't have taken the job if I'd known you were the boss," I admitted.

"Really?" There was a twinkle in his eye, which annoyed me. He seemed to think he could still do as he pleased with me. He was the same arrogant, selfish bastard he'd been in college. I never wanted to see it, always making excuses for him. My friends had called me out on it, but I always defended him. I learned the hard way. You couldn't trust him. Matthew Waterstone cared only about himself. It was all about him.

"Of course," I said, rather stiffly.

"But then we wouldn't be able to have any fun," he said, his voice low and flirty, his eyes glittering as he leaned forward to grab my wrist, caressing my arm with his thumb.

"No!" I said, a bit more firmly than I'd intended to, ripping my arm away. It had nothing to do with Dax though. Even if I was single, I would never hook up with Matthew again. Not after the way he'd treated me.

"Yes," he said and leaned in closer, his hand tightening around my wrist. I could feel the intensity in his grip, the intention in his touch. I stepped forward on his toe, hard. He exclaimed in shock and let go of my wrist.

I was completely unnerved by the whole exchange. I marched back to the table where the girls were laughing out loud now. "Way to go! You went right to the top, girlfriend! Grabbed the boss's ass!" Tash whistled to show how impressed she was. "I didn't know he was the boss!" I said, but I had to laugh with them. I gave it a few moments, waited for their attention to move on to something else before I quietly got out of there.

I needed fresh air. Fast.

I stood outside the bar for a few seconds, to calm down and organize my thoughts. How was this possible? How had I managed to end up at the same organization as Matthew? The one guy I never wanted to see again in my life. Ever again. I thought with sadness how much I had enjoyed the job so far and how I'd only been able to find it after months of searching. Where would I find another job like this?

The door swung open, and Matthew came out, smiling at me.

"After that little stunt of yours, I'm actually looking forward to Monday morning for a change."

He winked at me and walked off.

I had felt his glance slide over my skirt and my legs and thought of how I'd felt something that morning, almost a premonition that something would happen today. Despite everything, I couldn't help but feel pleased that I hadn't worn my jeans. He'd noticed my skirt and legs. I wanted him to know what he would never have ever again. Briefly, I felt my hand when it was on his behind, my palm burning. I rubbed my hand against my leg as if trying to rid myself of the feeling of his body.

But it only made it worse.

The feel of him on my skin.

Chapter 2

Matthew

I thought about Lauren all weekend.

While I was golfing with my boring cousin Evan and his brother-in-law, all through lunch at the dreary country club, listening to them drone on about new cars and expensive holidays, the cost of keeping their wives happy. A day of golf with Evan was something I had to suffer through occasionally on a Saturday. Another thing I had to do for the good of the company. His father and my father had started the company together decades ago. I had succeeded my father as CEO and Evan was heading up the International Sales Team.

And now, Lauren was working at Egal, too.

The last time I'd seen her was in college. This had to be three years ago. I had recognized her right away, though, she had hardly changed. Even though her hair was shorter now, she still had the bangs and those bright, blue eyes. There was the smile too, a dazzling and warm grin that drew people to her.

Seeing her again brought other things back to me. We'd had good times, my last year in college, going out with friends and playing tennis. Lauren was in college on a tennis scholarship, and she had a mean back hand. I wasn't half bad myself and we played quite often over the weekends, when we weren't out hiking or hanging out with some of her friends. Lauren was more sociable than I was, and I ended up falling in with her crowd on whatever jaunts they had planned. It was a carefree time of my life that I knew had to end. As it had. Leading the family company had always been the next step for me.

But when Lauren had felt me up at the drinks party on Friday, I had felt something that I hadn't felt in ages, interest, and amusement. I called the head of HR on my way home.

"Janine? Sorry to call so late... I wanted to check on a new hire?"

"Oh?"

"Lauren Lambert? In communications?"

"Let me think… I've already left the office. Let me think… Yes, that's right, our new Community Manager, I think? Everything all right?"

"I met her at the staff party now. She's young?"

"I sat in on one of her interviews. She had a lot of ideas and I think that swung it. For social media, youth is a big plus. We want to get her to push the vegan products."

I nodded. That made sense.

"We want to appeal to a younger demographic, right? Engage the younger consumer?"

"Absolutely."

I ended the call and thought about Lauren's reaction to seeing me again. The surprise seemed real, and she had not been pleased, I thought. I wondered if she would look for another job. I hoped not. I wanted to see her again. She looked good, sexy, with that tight, tennis body and those shapely legs.

On Monday morning, I sat through a few meetings, feigned attention in reports and feedback and bided my time until I could step out of my office and take the elevator down to the sixth floor. This was not the sort of thing I'd usually do, but I wanted to see her. I had spoken to the head of marketing and checked up on the role. Apparently, Lauren's predecessor had been away on maternity leave and then decided not to come back after all. As a result, there was a lot of work that needed doing in terms of social media, creating brand awareness on some newer product lines. Lauren had made a good impression on all at the hiring panel, and her energy and bubbly personality had counted in her favor.

I got out on their floor and saw her sitting at her desk straight away. Her dark hair fell to her shoulders, and she was wearing a bright red sweater that clung to her breasts.

"Lauren!"

She looked up, saw me, and blushed.

"Mr. Waterstone."

"Really? Mr. Waterstone?" I had to laugh, and she did too.

"I can't call you Matthew?" she said, looking uncomfortable. "Maybe I'll call you, boss?"

I considered that.

"So, you're not leaving the job then?"

She looked around, as if to check who was overhearing our conversation. The desk next to her was empty and the closest person was sitting with her back to us, too far to hear what we were saying.

"I don't want to," she said, looking down. "I like this job."

"Sounds to me like we need you too," I said, sounding rather flirty.

She looked uncomfortable and I liked putting her on the spot.

I decided to get out of there.

"Walk with me," I said, and walked to the foyer where at least we would be out of sight. She was wearing a tight skirt and high heels and looked good enough to eat. As soon as she came out of the office into the elevator lobby, I pulled her close enough to kiss her, my face inches away from hers.

"It's so good to see you again, Lauren. It really is."

It was good to see her. From the moment I had laid eyes on her again I could think of nothing else. I knew I wanted to kiss her, to put my mouth on those luscious pink lips, part them with my tongue. For a moment, I felt incredibly attracted to her. "Let's grab some lunch," I said, punching the button on the elevator.

"I... I ... must finish something," she said, looking over her shoulder.

"I'm the boss, Lauren," I reminded her with a wink as the door of the elevator opened. I got in and she followed.

We walked out to a food truck around the corner.

"Remember the pizzas we used to get in college? These are almost as good."

I bought us some pizza slices and we walked slowly, eating the hot food.

"Are you kidding? Those pizzas were terrible?! They always got our order wrong!"

I laughed. I had forgotten that. These days, that was the sort of thing that could really make me angry, but back then I could laugh it off. Thinking back to my former self, it occurred to me that I was more laidback back then, happier.

"So, how've you been?" I asked.

She glanced up at me, her blue eyes sparkling. "Since you dumped me, you mean?"

I shrugged.

"Let's just say, since college?"

"It's been... fine. My mom is still in the city, and I've been living with her."

I nodded. I also lived with my mother, and it was the last thing I wanted to discuss with anyone.

"And you like the job?"

"I love it!" she said quickly.

"So... you don't want to mess it up, right?"

I turned to face her. I wasn't going to kiss her on the street with God knows who was watching, but I did use my thumb to pretend wipe some sauce from her face.

"Keep your boss happy, right?" My voice was low, husky.

She stared at me.

"I have a boyfriend," she said, carefully.

"And he doesn't want you to make your boss happy?" I tried to make light of the conversation, but she turned away.

"What's wrong with you?" she hissed, stomping her foot in a rather adorable fashion.

I shrugged and had to laugh. The whole scene was charming, somehow, I couldn't see the harm in us hanging out together and I told her so.

"I have a girlfriend too, if that makes you feel better?"

"It does not!"

She stormed off in the direction of the office. I walked after her, amused by Lauren's reaction. When I got back inside, she was waiting for the lift, arms folded.

We weren't alone anymore. Other people joined us at the elevator, and we couldn't talk. We went up to her office and at her floor, I stepped out with her again.

I was determined to continue our conversation but when we got into her office, Diaz was waiting for her at her desk.

"Good, you're back," he said, frowning at a piece of paper.

"I want to talk to you about the email you sent earlier."

"Diaz," I said, and I saw him doing a double take.

"Mr. Waterstone! Everything okay?"

"Yeah, I was just welcoming Miss Lambert to the office."

"Right," he said, not sounding entirely convinced.

"I wanted to check about a tweet I saw last night," I said, making it up on the spot.

"Oh?"

"Is that the sort of thing I speak to her about?" I pointed to Lauren.

"Uhm, yes, sure," Diaz said, and sounded caught off guard.

"Maybe you haven't had time to go through the latest update from marketing?" I said, a trace of sarcasm in my voice. He was becoming more uncomfortable by the moment. I did sometimes take a secret pleasure in wrong-footing my employees. It kept them on their toes, stopped them from becoming too complacent.

"We've been getting some bad publicity about the Freezas product as you must know."

Neither of them knew what I was talking about. I could see it in their eyes, the frantic look that passed between them. I had expected the head of marketing, Tanya Chang, to talk to them about it, but it seemed she hadn't. Freezas was a frozen fruit lolly that was supposed to be sugar-free and without additives or colorants. But a child had fallen ill shortly after eating one and now everyone was blaming the product.

"This is your department. Communications is part of marketing, right?" I said, my tone serious. "You haven't been informed about the Freezas nightmare?"

"Uh, I'll check with Tanya," Diaz said and walked off quickly.

I found my good mood from earlier had evaporated. Instead, I was filled with irritation that the communications team had no idea what was going on with one of our big product lines.

"You don't have to have lunch with me if you don't want to," I said, rather coldly. "But you do have to be good at your job. That is a prerequisite for this position."

"I am good at my job," she said quickly, flushed.

"Are you though?" I let the words hang in the air.

I leaned forward and stared into her big blue eyes.

"Better than all the other thousands of pretty young things who come in here every day looking for a job?"

"I am good at what I do," she said again, sticking out her chin in a rather fetching attempt to be feisty.

"Thing is, Lauren. I don't like disappointment," I said. She bit her lip, and I could see the tip of her tongue nervously darting to her upper lip. "I really don't take disappointment well."

"I won't disappoint you."

"You did before though. Back in college? Seems to me rather convenient how you've forgotten about the lake party?"

She stared at me as if she couldn't believe I'd bring it up now.

"I think, Lauren, you will find that I have changed a bit since college. I am no longer able to forgive and forget, like I did back then. I mean, I let you off the hook rather easily, I'd say."

She just stared at me.

"I think you owe me, quite frankly."

She still didn't say anything.

"And I think you can begin by fixing this Freezas disaster. Right now."

I turned on my heel and marched out of the office.

Chapter 3

Lauren

As I walked back to our apartment, I became aware of the balmy late afternoon. Summer was coming to an end, and we were in for a lovely evening. I slowed down as I walked the streets to our place, noticing people taking strolls and eating ice cream and enjoying the atmosphere. New York in summer could be a glorious place. At the steps outside our apartment, I found my mother talking to one of our upstairs neighbors, Mrs. Penderis.

"Hey, honey!" my mom grinned at me. "I was hoping I'd see you tonight!"

I had been working late all week and often my mom was out or seeing friends by the time I got back.

"Can I get you a beer?"

"Sure."

I sat down on the steps, looked at the trees and families walking past. Two lovers, hand-in-hand, with eyes only for one another came by. I watched them, noticed how absorbed they were in each other's conversation, the way the woman threw back her head to laugh, the way the man's eyes lingered on her face. I remembered what it felt like to be that in love and rather wistfully wondered what happened to that feeling. Why couldn't love stay? Why did it seem like it always changed into something else or faded away?

"Here you go," my mom handed me an open beer and I took a grateful swig. It had been a long day and it felt good to be home.

"So, how's the new job? We've barely had time to talk this last week."

My mother had never looked like any of the other kids' moms when I was at school. She was always younger than the other mothers, always cooler. She felt more like a sister than a mother. She'd had me when she was quite young herself and it had always been just the two of us. Growing up, we'd been close and there had never been the kind of tension in the house that so many of my friends had. I always felt lucky, even though there was no father figure, no huge house or garden, no siblings to annoy or irritate me. We had our own world, and we co-existed happily together. My mom had been a model for a few years, then she'd had a few dead-end jobs before training as an art teacher, a job she loved and was good at. She saw it more as therapy than as a teaching job, a way of providing stressed kids with paint and equipment and an outlet for their many troubled emotions. Every now and then, there would be a kid with talent or a great idea for a project, and this would give her such job satisfaction.

"It's... good, great, really."

"You don't sound convinced."

My mom had been a part of my job search those months after I'd left college. She'd not pressured me to get a job, but I had taken the rejections personally. So many companies didn't even email back or send responses. I'd go to interviews and receive cold texts informing me that someone else had gotten the job. I started feeling something was wrong with me. I wasn't thin enough, or tall enough, or something. I'd started waitressing just to make a little money and feel less dependent on my mother. The job at Egal had come along as I was starting to give up hope. I loved the idea of running social media for a large corporation, being in charge of health products and especially vegan product lines. Everything had been going swimmingly until I'd discovered that Matthew was my boss.

I gave a sigh. "That's not it. It's my boss."

"What about him? He a prick?"

I had to smile; this was such a typical thing for my mother to ask. In many ways, she was my best friend. I decided to tell her what had happened. She listened to the whole story of how I'd felt his bum at the drinks party, laughing out loud when I discovered who the guy was.

Then when I told her about our lunch outing the next week, her face grew serious.

"Ok, that's not good. What are you going to do? Look for a new job?"

"I guess it wouldn't hurt to send out a few CVs again," I said, but I think she could hear my heart wasn't in it.

"How often do you have to see him?"

"I don't really deal with him at all," I admitted. "I report to my manager and there are like, I don't know how many people in the hierarchy after him."

She nodded, considering the situation. The beer had gone straight to my head, producing a nice mellow vibe. I leaned back against the side of the steps and closed my eyes.

"I don't really know much about Matthew," my mom said. "I mean I remember you dating a guy with that name, but did you bring him home?"

"Once or twice," I said. "Tall, good looking?"

My mom laughed, "Of course, he was! But was he the one that was a bit preppy?"

"Maybe."

I hadn't told my mom a lot about him, careful not to make too much of the relationship. My mother had always been a single mom and tended to be dismissive of men and boyfriends. I had grown up with the impression that men came in handy sometimes, like when you had to install a new TV or needed a plus one for a wedding. But when it came to living your life and planning your future, you had to put yourself first. My mother had bad experiences when it came to men and had been raised by my grandmother, a formidable woman I had only known for a few years before she died. She had apparently always said that men were more trouble than not, an expression my mother was fond of repeating. I never knew who my father was, only that she'd fallen pregnant during a fling and that she had wanted to keep me. I'd always felt loved and cared for and while it did bother me sometimes, I never quite had the guts to push her on the identity of my father. When it came to my own boyfriends, I tended to play down the seriousness of the situation. I knew my mom didn't want me settling down too early, she was always saying that I needed to get out as much as possible while I was young.

"He dumped me in his senior year," I said. "Right before he graduated."

"What an arsehole!" my always loyal mother exclaimed.

I smiled. "He was, rather. Jealous too, didn't like me hanging out with some of my friends. Accused me of fooling around with one of them, but I didn't."

"Of course not!" My mom was indignant. "I don't like the sound of him."

It was the part of him being jealous, I thought. It reminded her of a guy she used to date when I was younger. The relationship had been intense but when their fights became more vicious and he'd started breaking things, she'd ended it.

"And you think he's still interested? In you?"

I thought of the way Matthew had kept looking at me, standing too close to me, touching me. He was still interested, all right.

"Are you sure you're not?" my mom's voice changed. She knew me well.

"Definitely not," I said, sitting up straight. "I'm with Dax now, anyway."

"Dax," she smiled, drawing out the name in a drawl. She hadn't said much about him to me but I had the feeling she liked him. I also suspected that she knew our relationship wasn't that serious, that it was more about going out and having a good time together. Dax was a musician, he played bass for a band that was trying to make a name for itself in the city.

"Maybe just keep out of his way, then?"

"Yup."

My mom got up and got ready to go in. "What about soup for dinner? I told Mrs. Penderis I'd bring something by. I'll make extra. Tomato sound good?"

I nodded.

But I stayed sitting outside by myself for a little while longer.

Despite what I'd said to my mom, there was more to my and Matthew's break up. Our relationship had been going well all year. We never fought, almost never disagreed. Both of us were busy students and I had to train a lot with the rest of the tennis team, occasionally travelling for matches. I knew he came from an important family and that he had a serious job waiting for him after graduation. He'd often said that college was the only time of his life when he could pretend that his life was his own and that he could do what he wanted. He never took me home to his family and he'd explained that he wanted to keep me separate from them, as if they were contagious or something. I didn't question it.

Until the day we broke up, he'd never raised his voice or been mean to me. There was a certain coldness, an arrogance that I had found rather attractive initially. My friends didn't like him, some saying he was too haughty, too superior. But towards the end of the year, as he was beginning to wrap up his studies and prepare to go back to the city, he'd occasionally be short, dismissive. I made it off as being due to stress and the tension of graduation.

But then at the party, he'd lost it, accusing me of cheating on him and making a fool of him. Apparently, nobody made a fool of Matthew Waterstone. I had been so stunned by his tone, calling me names and being so unfair that I had not even tried to defend myself. It was ridiculous, really. I was sure he'd calm down the next day and apologize. But he hadn't. I was too proud to call him. I figured he could call me to explain himself. But he didn't do that either. I had been living with him in his student flat, even though I had my own room in a dorm across town. When I went back to our place, he had packed my things and left them in the living room with a note telling me to have everything out of there by the weekend.

I was stunned. He was talking to me like I was a servant, or a staff member like he probably had at home. Like I was someone who had to be dealt with, handled. I got my things and got out of there. But I was heartbroken. After a few days, when my anger and hurt pride had subsided, I found myself feeling confused. I had loved Matthew and I couldn't believe he would treat me this badly. He hadn't even given me a chance to explain anything. He would not pick up my calls or answer my texts. It was like I had ceased to exist to him.

I struggled with that. I couldn't just switch my feelings off and on like that. I couldn't believe that after our year together, he could move on just like that.

"Are you coming in?" My mom was calling me from a window. Seeing her face cheered me up. She'd always been able to do that. I may never have told her about how much Matthew had meant to me and how badly the break-up had affected me, but she knew something was up. Tomato soup was one of my favorite meals, a comfort food that she used to make when I was in high school after a bad day. She had a spicy Thai recipe, with red chili paste and coconut milk, extra mushrooms, and peppers.

I thought about the whole drama around the Freezas lolly, a healthy fruit treat. The kid who'd had an asthma attack, turned out to have accidentally eaten a cookie with peanuts in it at his school that day. His reaction had nothing to do with the lolly. After the comms department sent out a press release, I had a box of Freezas sent over to the boy's house and asked them to take pics of him eating the lolly. We then posted these on social media as damage control. It seemed to have worked. Other people posted pics of them eating their lollies, and it trended for a while. We got some good press and Diaz had been pleased with me. I hoped Matthew heard about it as well. But I had a feeling that would not make a difference. The last time he'd spoken to me, there had been a nastiness that reminded me of the last time I'd seen him in college.

A shiver ran down my spine.

The talk of me owing him and having to work hard not to disappoint him? I didn't like that. Even though he was as handsome as he'd been in college, there was something else there too. A hardness in his eyes, in his voice, that I did not remember. He was not the kind of guy you wanted as an enemy. Certainly, not me. I had an uneasy feeling about his last words to me earlier in the week, as if he intended to give me a hard time because I'd blown him off. Had he really expected me to fall into his arms, though?

Matthew Waterstone was a complicated man, I knew that. I had known that even in college, although back then, I was happy to think that his difficult side had to do with his family. When we were together, it could be just us. But it had never really been just us, I thought now. There had always been other people, other expectations, and pressures on our relationship. Warning signs I didn't want to see. I was a happy-go-lucky type of girl, someone who preferred to think happy thoughts and be positive. If I didn't pay attention to his bad traits, they weren't there. Something like that. I had been quite a bit younger then, more naïve. Even though I didn't want to admit it, Matthew Waterstone had broken my heart when he dumped me. I did not date anyone for a long time after that, spending the next year practicing tennis like I was preparing for the US Open. When I hurt my knee at the end of the next year, I had to quit the team and focused on my studies. I kept myself busy and my mind occupied. Slowly, my heart mended. But there was a weakness there and I needed to be careful now.

Especially around Matthew.

As I got up and went inside, I felt a bit of a chill for the first time that day.

Chapter 4

Matthew

The party at the Gillespie residence in Park Avenue was a formal affair. Our families had known each other for years and I'd grown up with Kyle, the youngest son. He'd come back from London recently and this was a welcoming party by his parents. It was known widely that Kyle had attended rehab and then some sort of retreat in Scotland, but that was not how his family described his time away. They referred to his "traveling". From my mother, I knew that Kyle's parents were hoping he'd step into the family business again.

"How long do we have to stay?" my girlfriend, Taya asked me, her lips barely moving. "I've had a terrible headache all day."

She was looking gorgeous, as usual. She was always one of the most striking women in any room. Apart from her height and incredible figure and bone structure, she had a certain bearing that separated her from most women. She'd grown up in an extremely wealthy family, the daughter of a hedge fund manager. She had only known privilege and comfort her entire life, so she knew how to play the game, appearances had to be kept up no matter how big the hangover was.

"Big lunch?" I asked, keeping my tone light.

I was rewarded with a small smile, barely perceptible to anyone else. "I wouldn't say, enormous, but yes, rather larger than usual."

"Anyone interesting?"

I wasn't really expecting her to tell me. I was making conversation, trying to pass time.

"Just the girls."

I nodded.

"I was thinking of going to France in the summer."

"Oh?"

"A few weeks probably."

Taya's parents owned a mansion in Provence. She liked to combine holidays there with shopping in Paris.

"Want to come?" She glanced at me, ever so casually.

"Sounds fab. It will depend on my schedule, though," I said, even though I couldn't really see myself taking off two weeks from work to lie in the sun. I had a feeling she knew I wouldn't come but felt she needed to ask.

"Waterstone! Thanks for coming!" It was Kyle, joining us. He put an arm around my shoulder, gave it a warm squeeze. Taya moved away to give us some time to talk.

"How're you doing?" I asked. Kyle looked well. He'd picked up a bit of weight since the last time I'd seen him, and his face had a healthy glow.

"Better," he winked at me.

Kyle and I had been at the same boarding school years ago and one night, getting high on some weed that one of our friends had smuggled in, he'd admitted to me that the pressure of the Gillespie name and family was too much for him. He didn't want to go into the automobile business and couldn't see himself working in an office all day.

I remember telling him that I didn't have a choice, that I had to do it. Since my father's death in a plane crash, I was the heir not only to the family fortune but the family business as well. My mother spent every waking moment reminding me how my office was waiting for me. I had no siblings while Kyle had an older sister who seemed keen to join the business. But she wasn't a son, Kyle had said, darkly. His father wanted him in the driving seat.

He had successfully avoided the pressure this far, first by going to college, then by going on some adventurer's challenge. He always had some plan or scheme to get out of his responsibilities. It had started to catch up with him, though, and before his stint in rehab, he apparently drove his car into a lake, coked up to the eyeballs.

"She's nice," he said, looking over at Taya, who was chatting to someone across the room. He pretended to shiver and looked at me pointedly. I smiled and shook my head. Taya came across as a bitch, but we understood each other. Most importantly, she knew not to have any expectations of me or our relationship. I could always call on her to come with me to these society events, where she knew what to say and what to wear. She got on with my mother, which helped too. As long as I didn't have to spend too much time in her company, we got along fine.

She wasn't Lauren, of course.

The thought popped into my head, rather unexpectedly.

Since finding out about her working there, I had started to play a rather naughty game at work with Lauren, messing with her head. I knew it was mean, but I enjoyed watching her trying to meet my crazy deadlines and insane requests. Putting team members under pressure was an old technique of mine and my executive team knew that. I made sure that Lauren wasn't the only one working long hours. Over the past week, I'd tasked her with creating positive buzz around a vegan product that had been launched a year ago but struggled to sell. The biggest problem was that we had a competitor with a similar product, which was not only cheaper but tastier too. I'd told Diaz that I expected Lauren to come up with a campaign that would help product sales increase by at least twenty percent. He'd looked very uncomfortable with those numbers, and I'd put him on the spot. Could they do it or not? If they weren't up to the task, then I'd find people who could.

I enjoyed the scramble that followed. I watched from the corridor as Diaz briefed Lauren, saw her outrage and then determination as she hunkered down behind her computer. There was a large screen in the foyer, and I could easily stand there watching the Communications department through the gap between the screen and the office. Within days, Lauren had managed to put up a video of an actress eating a sandwich made of our vegan cheese. Even though the actress was a former soap star, she was still well-known. Suddenly people talked about anti-aging properties of vegan food and a whole buzz was created in the media around how plant-based diets slowed down ageing. By the end of the week, sales for our vegan cheese had gone up by thirty percent.

On Friday afternoon, as the others started leaving the office, I called Diaz and told him I wanted a report on the week's social media campaigns as well as a breakdown of their figures before the end of the day.

Then I went home.

I received an email with the report at eleven o'clock that evening. I didn't even look at it. I didn't have to open it to know that Lauren was doing a fantastic job as community manager. I loved trying to think up new ways of making life difficult for her. Why, though? I hadn't spent a lot of time thinking about my motivation, even though I did spend a lot of time thinking about her. Maybe I was trying to punish her for filling my thoughts the way she had, making her pay for being less than keen to spend time with me.

Or maybe, there was more to it than that.

I was enjoying the idea of her working her heart out. It was to my benefit really, it was for me, indirectly. I was getting her attention, one way or another. I didn't think that she would quit. Every challenge I threw at her, she was able to meet and beat. She was even more efficient and creative than I thought she would be. It was as if she was accepting my challenges and saying, all right, I'll meet your bid and raise you one. A delightful game of mental poker.

I had not had as much fun at work in a long time.

It wasn't anything I could talk about to anyone though, not even Kyle.

"What'll you do now?" I asked him. We went outside and he lit up a cigarette. Summer was drawing to an end, and there was already a bite in the air. Still, I preferred this to the stuffy drawing room with all the guests wearing faked smiles while pretending interest in one another's conversations.

"My father says he'll cut me off if I don't join the firm," Kyle shrugged and smiled gamely. "I figured as much. Suppose I'll need to get a job."

"Doing what?" Kyle had never shown much interest in anything but partying and traveling.

"I figured I may take up sailing, do some racing, get some sponsorship."

"Sailing?"

Kyle nodded. "One my father's friends bought a yacht over in Monaco. He wants me to bring it back here. Guess I'll start off doing that."

"At least you won't have to worry about getting a place of your own then," I said with a laugh, slapping Kyle's back.

"Sounds like you've got it made!"

Kyle looked at me.

"You could come with me?"

"I wish!" I said with a laugh. The truth was that I didn't much like being CEO or running the company. But since Lauren had started working there, I had found myself looking forward to coming to the office for the first time in months. The long hours, the dreary meetings; all made worthwhile when I thought of her sitting at her desk a few floors below me, thinking of ways to meet my mad demands.

We stood in silence for a while. The party continued behind us and neither one of us seemed keen to go back in. It was the only life either of us had ever known, with not much choice as to the part we had to play.

Even though it looked like Kyle had found a way to get out of it, for now, it remained to be seen if he would be able to make a living off it. I could see my mother watching us from inside. Even from a distance, I could sense disapproval emanating from her. I knew she didn't like

Kyle and thought him weak and without purpose. She'd felt his parents had been too soft on him, made too many allowances. The subtext was always that I should not think I would be able to get away with that kind of behavior.

My relationship with my mother was tricky. After my father's death, she had been devastated. She spent a year locked in her room, heavily sedated while nannies made sure I got to school and ate my dinner. When she finally seemed to step back into the world, there was always a slightly vacant expression in her eyes, as if she had taken one too many sedatives. Then there was the smile that was always on her face. She was an attractive woman, still, and she'd inherited millions from my father's estate. But she was never interested in remarrying. She only cared about the family business. It was all about protecting my father's legacy and that was me. It was all on me. Ensuring my father had not died in vain, building a business and a family name that had to become one of the finest in the city. She became obsessed by it, and it was the only thing driving her. Without it, she would have no reason to live.

If I ever stepped away from the company business, I would destroy not only myself but her too, and the family business.

Chapter 5

Lauren

I was in the middle of something when Tash came over to my desk.

"Let's go for lunch," she said. "Come on."

I checked my watch; it was almost lunch time.

"I should really work," I said, keeping one eye on my screen. Work was so busy at the moment, it seemed like I'd just finished one deadline when another one came in.

"Yeah, about that," she said, looking at me pointedly. "Let's go!"

I looked over at Diaz's office, but he was engrossed in reading a report and didn't seem to notice. He wasn't that kind of a boss anyway and never said anything when we went out. I was feeling a bit jumpy about being away from my desk, though. Over the past two weeks, I'd been getting more assignments and I had a feeling it was coming from Matthew. It was a suspicion more than anything as Diaz was always the one to brief me and he would say it was a new communication strategy or that an idea had come from someone on the executive team.

"I heard something," Tash said, leaning over to me. "But let's not talk here. Let's go grab something?"

We went out into the street and Tash hooked her arm through mine. "We should do this more often, don't you think? Go for lunch?"

"Absolutely," I said with a smile. I liked Tash and enjoyed working with her. We were about the same age and similar in a lot of ways. She shared an apartment with her sister and was still single, dating several guys but not seeing anyone seriously. We sometimes went for coffee in the staff kitchen where she'd entertain me about her latest date, but this felt like something else.

We ended up getting sandwiches and walking to the park. It was lovely being out of the office, away from the glaring computer screen for a moment and I was enjoying the break. We found a bench and sat down to eat.

"I heard something yesterday," Tash finally said.

"I was under my desk, sorting out some of the cables. I think Diaz thought I wasn't in yet, because it was early, and I'd come in to beat the traffic. Anyway, I overheard him talking on the phone to Carol in Communications. He'd put her on speakerphone, so I heard both of them speaking."

I leaned in closer, Tash was speaking in a low voice even though there was no danger of anyone overhearing us.

"Carol said to Diaz that Waterstone was giving her such a hard time at the moment, she said he was all over the strategy documents and wanted presentations on every one of the products and brands and company lines!"

"Really?"

"She said she didn't know what was going on, because Waterstone apparently never cared about Communications or social media before."

I felt myself sitting up straight, taking a deep breath.

"What do you mean?"

"All of us have noticed it," Tasha said. "You've suddenly been given all this work. Why?"

"I... I ... assumed it's stuff that needs doing," I said lamely.

"You should have seen Melissa when she still had this job! She was always taking two-hour lunches, leaving early to go shopping! She put up a few tweets a day and that was it! There were no daily campaigns and Facebook pages and what not?!"

"Are you serious?"

I had been sure that Matthew was behind all the work coming my way, but I couldn't prove it. In the beginning, I'd enjoyed the fast pace and the sense that my job was deemed important to the company. But I'd barely finish one project when a new request fell in my lap. When I'd asked Diaz about it, he could only tell me it came from up top.

"Diaz asked Carol what was going on, he was worried that maybe Sweet Cheeks wanted to jack up Communications for some reason."

Ever since the night I'd grabbed his ass, Tash had called Matthew Sweet Cheeks. It was a harmless nickname, but I hated it. It reminded me of the whole stupid episode at the bar.

"But Carol said, no, it's all social media with him now," she looked meaningfully at me. "You know what that means... you!"

"I don't know," I said, uncomfortable.

"I think he likes you," Tash said, sitting back with a smug grin. "This is like in kindergarten, when a boy likes you and keeps trying to push you over or pull your pigtails. Sweet Cheeks is your garden variety toddler. Underneath that suit, and fancy haircut, he's still a five-year-old."

I had to smile.

I thought about telling Tash about my history with Matthew, but I was embarrassed about it. She would never believe that I hadn't known about his being the boss here when I'd applied for the job.

She leaned forward. "You had better watch out."

"Why?"

"Even five-year-olds are dangerous." She gave me a knowing look. "And I've heard stuff about him. Old Sweet Cheeks isn't that sweet."

"What do you mean?" I was very interested to hear her answer, but I couldn't look too keen.

"His family, it's all twisted and weird. He grew up with his mother, who's apparently mad as a hatter. His dad died in a plane crash when he was young, leaving everything to him. They're super rich and move in the top society circles. He's supposedly dating Taya de Soto, have you seen her?"

The name sounded familiar.

"She's gorgeous, the face of one of those big cosmetics companies, I forget which one."

"So, he's got a girlfriend, then," I said, trying to sound cool. "No problem."

"Big problem," Tash said quickly.

"Guy like Sweet Cheeks isn't going to want to date you. He wants to pin you against the wall!" she lowered her voice dramatically and grabbed my arm for effect. I had to laugh.

I wanted to tell her then that we used to go out in college, but I'd missed my chance. It was too late now.

"I'm serious! I think he got turned on by your stunt in the bar when you first joined."

"But why all the extra work?" I said, doubtful.

"He wants to see how much you can take, make you come to him," Tash suggested.

"You seem to know a lot about this!"

Tash shrugged. "I've dated a lot of men, believe me, this wouldn't even be the weirdest thing I'd heard of when it comes to office romances."

"I don't want anything to do with him," I said.

"Yeah, I reckon, he sleeps with you once and that's it, you're out the door," she said matter-of-factly.

"Have there been rumors of him and other women at the office?"

Tash thought about it. "Not really, but he does sometimes have favorites. People he suddenly calls on for work or to help him with stuff. For a while, their ideas are the best and all he'll listen to. Then, a few weeks, later, it's someone else again."

"He sounds temperamental," I said.

"I don't know... I think it's a stressful job. He was always groomed to be the heir, you know, the guy to take over from his father. Family members looked after it until he was ready to step in as CEO. Since then, all eyes have been on him to make it work and he has."

I nodded, taking it all in.

"He's always been nice enough to me," Tash said with a shrug. "But I'd watch my back if I were you."

It was a lot to take in. I struggled to concentrate on work that afternoon, Tash's words kept coming back to me and I hated it. I wanted the job to be about the work I was doing, not some weird tactic of Matthew's.

I didn't work late that evening.

Instead, I left on time and went home, got changed and headed out for an evening with Dax and some of our friends. I tried to relax, to enjoy the company and our conversation, but found that I couldn't. My thoughts kept drifting off to work and Matthew.

"What is up with you these days?" Dax asked as we went home. "You barely said a word all evening?"

I shrugged.

"It's this job, you should quit," he said.

"And do what?"

"Go back to waitressing, that's good money."

But I didn't want to be a waitress anymore. I liked handling social media for Egal, I wanted to be the community manager. It was not so much being part of a corporation, but I liked being able to handle the community aspect of the company. I believed in the products, and I thought I could help make a difference. I knew Dax thought I was selling out, becoming a boring office worker. When I talked about ideas I had for work, he was never really interested, and it was affecting our relationship. Everything was always about him.

"But I love this work. The vegan products Egal is promoting now are so cool."

Dax rolled his eyes. He'd never had much of an interest in health either and ate a burger almost every day.

"Can't we go just five minutes without talking about your job?!" he exclaimed. We'd walked back to his apartment, and I was going to spend the night there. We were standing outside his building, and I suddenly just wanted to go back to my own room and my own bed.

"I'm going to go home," I said.

"What? No, come on," he pulled my sleeve, trying to get me to come up.

"I'm tired and I've got an early morning," I said.

Dax looked at me and pulled his shoulders up. I could see something close in his face.

I took a cab home, feeling low.

As I walked into our apartment, my mom looked up from the couch where she was watching TV.

"Back already?"

"Not really feeling like being out tonight," I said.

She patted a spot next to her, inviting me to sit down next to her.

I knew that I could have told Dax the real reason for my worries about work. But then I'd have to talk about Matthew and our past relationship, and I wasn't ready for that. Dax and I didn't have that kind of relationship either. We didn't delve into our emotions or discuss our history, certainly not our former partners. I wasn't even always sure that he wasn't seeing anyone else while he was supposed to be with me either. I knew he got very drunk after some of their gigs when the band partied all night and I wasn't always with him. Dax was an attractive guy, and he had a hard enough time saying no to tequila and weed when he was partying. I did wonder if he'd say no to some of the groupies who were always hanging around backstage.

I snuggled up next to my mom and we watched some mindless reality tv. As per usual, we got drawn into the lives of these characters, arguing about what they were doing and wearing. It was an escape from real life, and I enjoyed thinking about someone else's problems for a bit.

Chapter 6

Matthew

When I came back from my morning run on Saturday morning, my mother was waiting for me in the kitchen. This was unusual. She wasn't up early as a rule, and we tended to avoid each other. Or, more accurately, I tended to avoid her. The house was split into different floors, she had the top half, and I had the bottom. The kitchen was a communal space but since she never ate and I usually came home late from work, we hardly ever saw each other.

"I've made coffee," she said. She was dressed in a silk blouse and pressed pants, her hair set perfectly, not a strand out of place.

"Thank you."

I took some water from the fridge and waited.

She leaned against the counter and folded her arms, waiting for me to finish.

"Is there something I can help you with?" I asked, a bit impatiently.

"What are you up to this weekend?" she asked lightly. "I was wondering if you would join me on Sunday for lunch at my club."

"Why?"

"Can't a mother have lunch with her son? I haven't seen you in ages," she said in a slightly plaintive tone that I hated. "Also, I wanted to talk to you."

"About what? Can't we talk about it now?"

I had to fight back my annoyance. Over the years, my mother's emotional fragility had become an irritation. For years, after my father's death, I'd been told how vulnerable and weak she was, how she couldn't be expected to attend sporting events or go away on holiday with me. While in boarding school, I had to spend almost all the holidays with my insufferable cousins or be locked up in this house with some nanny. When I saw my mother, it would be for an hour of two, when she'd have a vacant, vague air about her that I later came to realize was caused by the tranquilizers she took. I had agreed to move into this house following graduation but only if we could have separate living quarters.

My mother smiled sadly.

"You are always so busy, I thought we might have a nice lunch and talk about the future."

"I'm supposed to go out to Kyle's on Sunday," I said, even though I had no such plans. "What about the future?"

"You and Taya. I want to talk about setting a date."

I put down the bottle of water and got myself some coffee. This topic of conversation required something stronger.

"Why now?"

"You've been together almost a year now, right?"

"Yes."

"And you're happy together?"

I nodded.

"Then I think it is time to start thinking about the next step, don't you? Wedding plans take time and I'm sure she will have a very specific idea of what she wants."

I tried to think of the best way to respond.

"You're not getting any younger, you know?" my mother said.

"And Taya won't wait around forever," she warned. Then she added, "Her mother and I had tea earlier in the week, she mentioned they were going to France in the summer. She also said it was quite a lovely spot for a wedding."

It all made sense now. The mothers had been plotting and Taya and I were expected to simply toe the line.

"I am not sure that Taya and I are at the point where we are ready for marriage," I said.

"But you have spoken about the future, together, haven't you?" my mother asked, with more emphasis. When she had introduced me to Taya months ago, she had made a point of telling me how suitable we were for each other, both of us from good families with established means. She liked Taya's bearing and manners, she had on many occasions pointed out how well she would fit into our family. She'd invited Taya for lunch and on shopping outings, informing me afterwards how pleased she was with Taya.

I gave a sigh. "I'm not ready to get married, Mother."

"Matthew." Her voice was dangerously soft. "You must get married. You know this. It is your duty. To your father, to me. To this family!"

My mother's voice was rising.

"Mother," I tried to calm her down.

"It is the only thing you must do! In this life! It is the only thing I have ever asked of you!" Her eyes were wild, wide open, her hands shaking as she gesticulated wildly. I thought she might have a stroke.

"Mother, please! Calm down!" I walked up to her, grabbing hold of her arms.

She blinked a few times and seemed to come to herself, then wrenched free from my grip. She took a few shallow breaths.

"This is all I have ever asked of you!" She had turned to face me again, her eyes burning coals of fire.

"To do your duty to this family! Do you think you can find it in your spoilt, rotten heart to do that?!" she spat the words out like poisonous darts.

"Yes." There was no other answer to give.

She glared at me one final time before turning away and walking up the stairs.

I had to sit down after that. It had rattled me, I had to admit that. Scenes with my mother were rare but when they happened, they were deeply unsettling. Her emotional state had always overshadowed everything else. I had so little memory of my father. He was always working, always off on some trip. Then, one day, he didn't come back. But that accident had really cost me both my parents. The depression that overtook my mother after my father's death, plunged her into a deep, dark hole and nothing seemed to help. She went from one hospital to another, one retreat to the next. I went off to school and whenever I came home, I was always told not to upset my mother, to be as agreeable as possible. I would sit by her bed, and sometimes she would tell me stories of my father, of his dreams for the company and the things he wanted to do; all the things I would do in his stead as soon as I could. "You will finish what he started," was one of her favorite sayings.

I thought of what she wanted me to do. Marry Taya.

That had never been a part of our bargain.

I thought back to the party we'd gone to for our first date. It was a fashion thing, aboard a cruise that paddled along the harbor while everyone got completely hammered. I remembered being introduced to Taya and being pleasantly surprised to see how good-looking she was. A stunner. My mother had mentioned that she was a beauty, but that didn't necessarily mean I would agree with her. Taya was tall and curvaceous, with sexy hips and a pair of surgically enhanced breasts. Her golden blonde hair fell almost to her hips and with those slanted eyes, she had an almost aristocratic appearance.

"Call me Taya," was the first thing she said to me. "Everyone else does."

We got on right away, the conversation flowed and there was no need to fill the silences. When I mentioned our parents being keen on us getting together, she'd rolled her eyes. "Ticking their boxes, you know?"

Then she said, "I have no problem with that though, us seeing each other, making it formal?"

"Oh?"

"I feel I should point something out, though," she said, matter-of-factly. "I'm what you might call asexual. Not really interested in sex. Obviously, you may be, and I don't mind you getting your kicks elsewhere, as long as you are discreet."

I was rather disappointed. I'd rather looked forward to seeing what Taya looked like underneath the make-up and the fake tan and body sculpting underwear. I would too, in due course, get to see it all. Taya didn't mind me spending the night occasionally, but there was no sex. She was serious about that. Not with me, anyway. But that I would only find out about later. Taya viewed her body like an instrument of a vehicle. It had to be maintained and looked after, a little like a car, which got you to places, and made life easier.

But marry her?

I didn't think she wanted to marry me any more than I wanted to marry her.

But I wondered if she would do it if there was enough pressure from her parents. I tried to imagine a life with her and couldn't. I knew she couldn't help it, that Taya was a product of her environment and upbringing, but the result was a lifelike mannequin who had no spark of life in her. No spontaneity, no joy or pleasure. Taya looked perpetually bored, unimpressed with everything and everyone around her.

I thought of Lauren and the way she had laughed when I reminded her of the pizza we used to eat in college. She'd thrown back her head and given a rolling, deep laugh.

For a few moments, I was lost in thoughts of Lauren and an awareness that when I was around her, I felt unlike I did with anyone else. I found her funny, and I wanted to hear what she said next, her views were interesting. I liked the way she was responding to my insane work requests, taking it all in her stride. I could see Diaz was thrown by it, worried that I might somehow be questioning his management style or results, but it was all about Lauren.

I knew I had to speak to Taya and warn her about what our parents were up to. I wondered if they had spoken to her and how she had reacted. We needed to have a plan on how to cope with it. I was sure that Taya would feel the way I did. I couldn't imagine Taya with babies and diaper bags. Surely, it would be the last thing that she wanted.

Because marrying Taya was absolutely the last thing that I wanted.

Chapter 7

Lauren

After work one day, I got a text from a friend.

R U going to the gig at Lulu's tonight?

I had no idea what she was talking about. Dax and I were still not speaking after our row the other night and I'd been keeping myself busy with work. But after a long day of staring at websites and product pages, reading people's comments and trying to come up with winning ideas, I was ready to let my hair down and relax. Going out sounded good and Dax and I needed to talk anyway.

Yeah, meet u there?

I got a thumbs-up on the text and felt my mood lift. I was looking forward to going out and forgetting about Matthew and my unbelievable work schedule.

When I got home, the music was playing loudly, and my mom was in her room. There were clothes all over her bed and her wardrobe doors were wide open.

"I've got nothing to wear!" she exclaimed, pointing at the clothes strewn around her. Her hair was wet, and she had a towel wrapped around her body.

"Going on a date?" I guessed with a smile.

My mom rolled her eyes. "Let's just call it dinner."

"Who's the guy?"

She looked at me with a smile. "He's just... this ...guy. You know..." she said, not wanting to talk about it. I knew my mom well enough to know that she liked him too much to jinx the date by talking about it. It had been a while since there had been someone in her life. Since she broke up with her last proper boyfriend almost two years ago, she'd barely been out.

My mom was still an attractive woman. She was still young, 45, and she looked good, having watched her figure. She still wore her hair long and dyed the gray out and I thought she could pass for a woman in her thirties any day. She'd never struggled to attract attention, but she quickly grew bored or annoyed with the men in her life. She felt they became controlling or demanding. She was free-spirited and independent and liked her own space. I had liked her last real boyfriend, a vintage car salesman called Hank. He wanted the two of them to move in together into their own place, build their own life. He was divorced with two grown children. My mother liked him, but I could see her becoming antsy at the talk of looking for a flat for the two of them, discussing building features and the advantages of certain neighborhoods over others. She felt he was moving too fast. After all these years of being on her own, I wasn't sure that she could commit to anyone else.

"Are you going out tonight?" she asked.

I nodded.

"Seeing Dax?"

I didn't volunteer any more information and went to take a shower. I put on some skintight jeans and high heels, glamming it up. I was in a strange mood. As I put on make-up, applying eye liner, and painting my lips red, I wondered about Dax and thought about our relationship. We didn't have a history of deep, meaningful talks. Whenever we had a disagreement in the past, we usually waited for it to blow over. Neither of us liked conflict and sometimes I wondered if we didn't care enough about our relationship to really fight for it.

I left before my mother did, giving her a peck on the cheek to wish her good luck. She looked lovely, in a long, boho dress and a jean jacket and boots. "You look terrific," I said. "He doesn't stand a chance."

"So do you!" she exclaimed. "Going for the biker chick look?"

Maybe I was.

Lulu's was a relatively new club in town and for the band to have booked a gig there was a big deal. By the time I arrived, there was a quite a line outside and I had to queue to get in. Inside, there were many people. The lighting was low and there were laser lights making it hard for me to spot Dax or any of the band members. I looked for my friend but couldn't find her. Another group was still playing, and the music was blaring. I made my way through the dancing crowd and found a place at the bar to order a drink.

I spotted Dax on the other side of the bar, talking to a young woman. She was young and pretty and they were standing very close together. I walked around to the other side of the bar to get a closer look. I needn't have worried about them noticing me as the two of them were deeply engrossed in their conversation. Dax was sitting on a bar stool and the girl was standing between his legs, very close to him. The scene was intimate, there was no mistaking their closeness. The girl's face was pleading, and she put her hand on his thigh, quite high up.

I felt my heart turn to lead.

At that moment, Dax turned his head and saw me. I saw his eyes widen, an expression of shock. He jumped up, shrugging off the girl who stepped away, dismayed.

"Lauren!" He came up to me.

"I didn't know you were coming!"

"I can see that," I said, crossing my arms.

"We're about to play…. We're next on, I was just grabbing a drink," he was blabbing. "Did I tell you about the gig tonight?"

"I felt like coming out," I said. "Watching you play. I always watch you play, don't I?"

"Not lately," he said. "Lately, it's been all about the job."

"At least you found someone to keep you busy," I said, sarcastically indicating the girl who seemed to be waiting for him at the bar.

"Oh, that, that's Mandy, she's just a friend."

"A friend?"

I didn't know what to make of Dax or the way he was trying to pretend nothing was going on with him and this Mandy. I saw that we'd been drifting apart a lot over the past few weeks and I didn't know what was keeping us together anymore, if I even wanted us to be together anymore.

"I'm glad you came," he said, stepping forward, close enough to kiss me. I could smell him, a mixture of whiskey and smoke and old leather jacket.

"Are you now?" I said, still sarcastic.

He seemed to lose his temper then.

"Shit, Lauren! What do you want from me?"

"What about a little honesty?" I said, sharply. "Or is that not rock-and-roll enough for you?"

We were having a full-blown fight in the middle of the club, but it was so noisy that nobody seemed to hear. It was liberating, somehow, being able to say exactly what I was thinking and knowing that the party was going on around us.

"You want honesty? I'll give you honesty," he said, his voice shaking with anger. "How about how you've changed since you've gotten this job? I don't recognize you anymore. You've become this corporate clone all about the money and the page clicks! It's fucking boring!"

"You mean caring about my job? About something more than you for a change? Is that why you had to go out right away and find someone else to sit at your feet and stare adoringly at you on stage?"

"Fuck you," he snapped. He was angry, I'd pushed him too far. But I was angry too, fed up with having to pretend I was dating a rock star when he was just another average musician with a massive ego that needed constant massaging.

"No, fuck you," I said.

I turned around and marched out of the club.

I knew it was over between us, there was no way back from the fight we'd just had. Then there was this girl, Mandy, and I knew there was something going on between them.

I felt incredibly lonely suddenly. This was not how I wanted this evening to go. I'd been looking forward to switching off, to seeing my boyfriend, and have a few drinks, maybe dancing and staying up late. I had not wanted to have a fight with Dax, to say things I didn't want to. I knew it was the job, the stress of the past few weeks getting to me. It hadn't helped that I'd seen that girl all over Dax, knowing they were probably far closer than they should be.

I went home and found our apartment dark and quiet. I got into bed and pulled the covers over my head, wanting to sleep and forget about the whole bloody evening. By the time I got up the next morning, my head was throbbing with a monster headache. I got dressed and dragged myself off to work.

I was in a bad mood and feeling rotten. I avoided the others, getting coffee and settling down to work at my computer. I checked my emails and started doing my usual sweep of social media updates. There were some Facebook pages going live for some of the products and I had been supervising the process with the designers and the developers. There had been a rush to finish the project as management apparently wanted the pages live by the end of the week. There was still a bit to be done and I pushed myself all day to finish writing the copy and get the pages ready. I worked through lunch, enjoying the pressure of the deadline to take my mind off other things.

Then, at around three o'clock, Diaz called me into his office.

"Turns out we're not going live after all with the Facebook updates."

"What?"

I couldn't believe my ears.

"I just heard. There was a meeting upstairs...Carol met with the CEO, I think. They're rethinking the individual pages."

"Are you kidding me?!" I thought my head was going to explode, like in one of those cartoons. The fury building up in me was frightening. I had suggested one page for the brands and had been told to instead build individual pages for each product in the brand line. It had been a staggering amount of work, and now, like that, they were having "a rethink?"

"This is good news, right?" Diaz was trying to calm me down. "At least, you can go home and have a weekend. No need to rush anything through today."

I thought of the weekend ahead, two days of thinking about nothing but my failed relationship and my horrible job. It was all too much.

I walked out of Diaz's office and straight past my computer.

"Hey, where are you going?" Tash asked me as I walked past her desk.

"I'm going to have a little chat with Mr. Sweet Cheeks," I said.

"What?"

I knew I was crossing a line, that I was about to do something I would regret. But I didn't care anymore. I'd been pushed too far, and I'd had enough.

I stood at the elevator and pressed the button. Tash came after me.

"Wait!" she called, but the elevator opened, and I got in, closed the doors.

On the executive floor, I got out and walked straight to Matthew's office. I knew which one it was. It was at the end, a big glass structure with a huge area outside for meetings and who knew what else. I walked straight past the personal assistant who tried to stop me.

"Wait! Who are you? Do you have an appointment?"

I could see Matthew in his office, talking on the phone. I didn't knock on the door but walked right in. The secretary followed closely behind me, trying to talk me out of going in but I ignored her. Matthew turned around and saw me, frowned, and ended his call.

"I'm sorry Mr. Waterstone, she barged right in!" his frightened PA said.

"That's right," I said. "I have a bone to pick with you."

Seeing him sitting there in his designer shirt with his bottled water and his expensive watch ticking off the minutes of his day in exquisite detail made me angrier than before. It was like he was better than anyone else, sitting up here in his glass tower stepping on other people's lives in his exquisitely handmade Italian shoes.

"Can it wait?" he asked, sounding so civilized and polite that I thought I would physically attack him.

"I'm afraid it can't." I said, trying to copy his tone.

He stared at me and said to his PA, "You know, Wanda, it's fine. Let me deal with this."

"But, what about your..."

"Cancel it, or move it, I don't care," he said curtly. "You go home, and I'll deal with this. It's important."

His secretary nodded and left. Matthew got up and closed the blinds on his office windows to give us some privacy. Then he walked over to the cabinet and said, "Drink? I know I need one." Then he went ahead and poured us each a glass of something strong.

He motioned for me to sit down on the couch in his office. He handed me one of the glasses and said, "So, what's up?"

I hadn't expected him to act like this.

He was being so friendly, so accommodating.

I sat down and gathered my thoughts.

Chapter 8

Matthew

College was the best time of my life.

Without a doubt.

For the first time in my life, I was the same as everyone else. The school I had chosen was upstate, far enough from the city and everyone I knew. It had an excellent business school and an author I admired was a lecturer there. My mother was initially unhappy about my choice, she'd have preferred a better-ranked institution. But it didn't matter, ultimately. I insisted and she gave in, reminding me that it was only for a few years and that I would have to come back to the city, take my place in my father's office.

I knew that.

So, I made the most of the little freedom I had. I found an apartment near campus and then advertised for a roommate, not because I needed the money, but so that I would blend in easier. I wanted, for once in my life, to be ordinary. To see what it was like. The guy who took the room was a business major like me, and we became friends. Warren was a farm boy from Pennsylvania and upon graduation, he'd have to go back to his daddy's fields and a life of getting up before dawn every day to feed the chickens and watch the wheat grow. He was determined to sow his wild oats while he could and I was happy to go along with him, attending every keg party and foreign film festival I could. I'd met a few girls along the way, but I was careful not to get too close with any of them.

Then I met Lauren.

We'd met at a college sports day. I'd gone along with Warren who wanted to watch the football. I was wandering around the fields when I heard Lauren and some team-mates laughing. They had finished their games and even though they'd lost, they seemed to be in high spirits. They looked cute in their tennis whites and the short skirts, but Lauren was the one who caught my eye. There was something about her that set her apart from her mates, the way she laughed and talked to them. She had a wonderful smile. I went up to talk to them about their matches and the girls invited me to a party. I went only to find Lauren and to ask her out. We became a couple soon afterwards. Something clicked between us and after a few weeks, when usually I would have broken off any relationship, I found myself wanting to stay with her a bit longer.

When the holidays came, I told her things were complicated with my family and I'd assume she'd complain about not seeing me for a few weeks. But I was wrong. Lauren accepted that we'd be apart and made plans with friends. I was relieved. It meant I could keep college and my city life separate for a little while longer.

I couldn't wait to get back to college, though. Those few months with her during my final year were the highlight of my college years. Lauren knew so many people and was always doing something fun. Whether it was camping in the mountains or apple picking when the season came, she was always off to some festival or another. I'd never met anyone so spontaneous or outgoing. The end to our relationship came suddenly and far sooner than I'd wanted it to. I had a plan worked out for how I could somehow maintain contact with her after I left college, but then the whole lake party happened.

When she started working here, I felt my initial attraction to her spark up again. I didn't like that. After what she'd done to me, I should have been able to cut her out of my life without hesitation. I'd allowed myself to become too emotionally involved with her and that had cost me. I was still angry with her and with myself as well, for the way our relationship had ended. I liked being able to punish her now, even though it was three years later. I guess I knew I wasn't over her exactly.

But when she came into my office that afternoon, I could see it was too much. I'd gone too far. She wasn't looking well, wasn't her usual radiant self. She was wearing jeans and some sweater instead of one of her usual interesting outfits and her hair was hanging down limply. I made us a drink, invited her to sit down, to talk to her. She had come in in quite a huff but as soon as she sat down, it almost evaporated. I had to coax her to talk to me.

"I've had enough," she suddenly said. "I quit."

"What do you mean?" I said, shocked. I hadn't expected her to give up so easily.

"Oh, please. As if you don't know."

She wouldn't say any more than that but finished her glass and held it out for a refill.

I had to think of something, I couldn't let Lauren walk out of the office, and my life, like this.

"I really don't," I put on my most sincere voice. "What's going on?"

She rolled her eyes. "You put the Facebook product pages on hold? We were going live today?"

"Yes? And?"

"I've been working myself to death on those pages for the past week! After telling you I didn't think it was the right move. I put my life on hold, lost my boyfriend and then at three o'clock this afternoon, I hear, oh wait, maybe I'm right?"

She broke up with her boyfriend? I decided not to pick up on that right away.

"What do you mean you worked yourself to death? You have a team right, it's not just you?" I knew full well that she was working social media by herself.

"What team?" she snorted. "It's just me and you know it!"

"But what about Tash and that other girl? Petra?"

"They are part of Communications!"

I put on a shocked face. "I thought they were helping you on the social media project. It's a lot of work!"

She pulled a face. "Please, like I don't know it."

"I'm sorry," I said, showing as much contrition as I could. "I really didn't want to put you through all that." I put on my most sympathetic face, leaning forward to touch her hand.

"Bullshit," Lauren said flatly, not having any of it.

"Look, it's fine. I gave this everything and now you can take it and shove it." She got up and got ready to leave. This was one of the things I liked about Lauren, her ability to let things go. I had enough obsessive neurotics in my life, to know that Lauren was not one of them.

"Wait!" I said. Her hand paused on the door.

"You're right. I knew you were working alone."

She turned around and walked back to me. She was looking at me differently now, a more calculating look in her eyes.

"I wanted to get back at you," I said. I was trying a different tack now, defense. I had no idea if it would work, but it was worth a shot.

"For what?"

"For college, cheating on me," I tried to shrug it off like it meant less to me because it happened so long ago.

"Cheating on you?" She repeated the words. "I didn't cheat on you."

"With that guy, what was his name? Gabriel?" As if I'd ever forget his name.

"Gabriel?" She stared at me. Then she laughed. "I never cheated on you with Gabriel. As if I could, he's gay!"

"Gay?" I was losing my footing here.

"You thought I cheated on you with Gabriel?! Is that why you broke up with me?"

"I found you two together in bed at that lake party! Remember? I had a test that day and said I'd come later but then missed my ride. By the time I got to the house, I couldn't find you and then when I did, well...."

I had buried the memory of that weekend deep in the recesses of my mind. I never thought of it. Remembering the pain and the betrayal that she had caused still managed to upset me.

Lauren shook her head, incredulous. "We shared a bed, yes, there weren't enough beds for everyone. But that doesn't mean we slept together! You got so mad, wouldn't let me explain. I thought you were angry about me leaving without you!"

I remember that I was so shocked at finding her in bed with someone else that I could barely talk to her. I was too freaked out. Perhaps deep down I'd always expected her to let me down somehow. After all, that was what everyone in my life had always done. I had not given her time to explain. I had left and not seen her again. I had graduated then anyway, and it was a clean break. This was how I justified it to myself.

"Gabriel is gay?"

"So gay!" Lauren laughed. "Back in college he was dating two guys at the same time and was constantly struggling to decide which one he had to be with!"

"So, you never cheated on me?"

I sat back on the couch, which was hard as wood. Why on earth did I have such uncomfortable furniture in my office? It was some top designer's showpiece; I knew that much. But right then, I wanted something comforting, not about to break my back.

"I loved you Matthew," Lauren said, simply. "Why would I cheat on you?"

She had no problem saying that. It occurred to me that things were very different for her, the world so much less murky. I was surrounded by people motivated by all kinds of hidden desires and twisted needs. But Lauren wasn't like that. She was honest and direct.

"I felt the same about you," I said slowly, not able to use the word as she had. "I think that was the problem."

"How could that be a problem?"

"For me," I said. "Love is vulnerability, weakness, giving power away. I always have to be in control. Or fake being in control at least."

"I'm glad I don't have to be you," Lauren said with a sigh.

There was a pause.

"Stay on. I will give you two interns to help you on the social media pages," I said. "They can start on Monday. And no more crazy deadlines. I'll meet with you instead of going through all these other people. That way I know exactly what's going on."

"I don't know." Lauren looked uncertain.

"You've been doing excellent work, your grasp of the market and how to position our products is fantastic. You should see how sales have gone up on those specific ranges. It is remarkable."

She smiled sadly.

"Think about it," I said.

She looked at me and I saw her thinking about more than just staying. I saw her looking at me and felt her thinking about me, about us. I didn't think twice, I leaned forward and kissed her. It was a daring move; a risk and I acted without thinking about it too much. She didn't move, and I pulled away, but not too much.

"Your boyfriend is an idiot for letting you go," I said in a low voice.

"All the men in my life are idiots," she said with a crooked smile and then she kissed me back. This time, there was no hesitation. I could feel the heat coming off her skin and it felt like it was setting me on fire. It had been a long time since I'd wanted anyone that much. I kissed Lauren deeply, holding her face between my hands and feeling her hands slipping in underneath my shirt. She was pushing me closer, against her. I was uncomfortably aware of my erection in my pants, the bulge pressing against her. She felt it too, breaking away from me long enough to give me a sly smile. Her hands went down to my belt buckle, undoing it and slipping her hand into my underwear. Feeling her against my skin, I was flooded with incredible sensations of pleasure. She pushed me back into the couch, then leaned over and pulled my cock free from my pants, licking the tip with quick, darting movements that sent me crazy with desire.

"Wait," I panted, taking off her top and bra, caressing her gorgeous breasts, rubbing my hands over her nipples until they hardened. She took off her pants and I barely had time to notice her shaved pubic hair as she opened her legs and I found her ready, wet, and warm. I put my arm around her and lifted her onto the couch so that I could have more freedom to move against her, to feel her move with me. I didn't want it to be over too quickly, but it had been a while since I'd felt this intense physical desire for anyone. Her hands were on my back, slipping lower onto my ass, and I felt her nails dig into my skin as she pushed me deeper into her. It drove me wild, and I felt myself thrusting harder and deeper. I couldn't keep myself back anymore even though I wanted to prolong the pleasure. I looked at Lauren, her mouth opening in ecstasy as I pushed myself deeper into her. She arched her back and I felt myself giving it to her, as hard as I could, and when we came, we came together. I held her close, her body as sweaty as mine.

Chapter 9

Lauren

It happened so quickly.

All of it.

Then it was over and I felt deeply, deeply embarrassed.

He pulled away from me and we sat up, slowly putting our clothes back on. I was very aware of being in his office, the boss's office, and the fact that we had had sex in his office like the worst kind of cliché. I wondered if he'd done this sort of thing before and with whom, which hardly helped. I couldn't wait to get out of there.

"See you Monday?" I mumbled and didn't wait for an answer before letting myself out of his office.

So much for my efforts at quitting.

But to be honest, I hadn't really wanted to quit. I had wanted to confront him about what was going on at work and had gotten him to admit that he was doing all of it on purpose. He'd apologized, and then came the explanation of why he'd done it. All the work assignments, the impossible deadlines. I couldn't believe that the real reason he'd broken up with me in college had been about Gabriel. Sweet Gabriel, who had been the best friend in the world to me. It had never even occurred to me that Matthew could feel jealous or left out of our friendship.

There had been so many times when Matthew had gone home to his family, when I hadn't felt like going back to the city. My mother often had to work, and I didn't feel like being alone in the flat all day. Gabriel and I ended up going on all kinds of adventures. We'd hitchhike to California or join friends on a rock-climbing expedition. Gabriel and I were close, but it was never romantic, he was like a brother to me.

I felt exhausted.

It had not been a good idea to sleep with Matthew, I knew that and it should not have happened. But it did. I had been so emotional after the break-up with Dax and all the work I'd been doing. The energy between us had been weird. It was all anger and frustration at first and somehow, talking about our past relationship had brought back the feelings I'd had for him. I seemed to have forgotten how he broke my heart, pushed me aside.

I was now truly in a foul mood.

When I got home, I was glad to see my mom was out. I spent the evening watching TV and pushing all thoughts out of my head. There was a bottle of wine in the fridge, and I drank all of it by myself, welcoming the haze that descended after my second glass. I spent Saturday doing laundry and helping my mom clean our apartment. By the evening, I was ready to go out and texted Melony, one of my friends.

Do u wanna go out? My treat?

Sure. Where?

Let's start with pizza. Usual place.

Cool.

I offered to pay because I knew Mel was battling with her finances. She had a job at an advertising agency, but the position was very junior, and the money was terrible. She'd been looking for something else for some time, but nothing had come up yet. Mel was one of my more recent friends and she knew several of Dax's friends as well. I wanted to ask her what was going on and fortunately, I didn't have to wait too long for her to talk about it. Halfway through her first beer, she said, "I heard about you and Dax."

"Who told you?"

She seemed to think. "Nolan maybe?" The band's manager. "I was really shocked, you guys seemed so solid."

I would not have used that word to describe us, I thought.

"Did you know about him and that girl?"

"Mandy?" Mel seemed to shift in her seat. "I think she's one of the girls who's always around, you know, a groupie."

"But her and Dax?"

"I don't know," she said.

"Dax told Nolan that he'd made a mistake breaking up with you." She looked at me meaningfully. "So, he obviously still cares."

I thought about that. While it was nice to hear that, I wasn't sure how I really felt about that. Did I want Dax back? After everything that had happened? I was also upset that he was so uninterested in my job and what it was about. It had felt good when Matthew had said that I had done well with the social media, that my campaigns had driven up profits. I wanted my job to mean something, to spend my time making a difference. I knew this was something Mel would understand. She also wanted a job that she loved, cared about.

"Have I ever told you how I got so into social media?" I asked her. She shook her head.

"It was in college. There was this girl who lived on campus. I didn't know her but one day, she posted in an online forum about how this guy was stalking her. She said she'd gone to the police, and they said there was nothing they could do, and she was really scared."

"That's terrible!"

"Yeah. Anyway, she managed to find a picture of him and posted it online. Then someone else recognized the picture as belonging to a guy who had stolen his backpack with his laptop from campus. He went to the police, and they opened a case. They went looking for this stalker guy, and when they searched his apartment, they found loads of stolen stuff. Turned out he was this serial burglar, and he was charged and brought to trial."

"Wow, that's amazing."

"He had some priors, so he got jail time. Even though he wasn't prosecuted for the stalking, at least he was taken off the street and the girl could finish her studies without him bothering her. That case really got me thinking, you know, how nobody was able to help this girl but through social media, a way was found to get this guy out of her life."

"Not to mention, stop him from stealing from all those people!"

"Exactly!"

I got us another round of drinks. "I saw how powerful the medium is. People think we escape through social media, but really it is connection and often, a very judgement-free way to connect with people. "

"And you are using social media now to promote this company you're working for?"

I was glad she asked. I wanted to talk about Egal.

"This is what Dax never understood. It's not about the company or making money for the guys in suits. It's about spreading awareness about cool vegan products. There is so much stuff on the market now and the company hasn't done specific advertising for their vegan range."

"What is their flagship product?"

I rolled my eyes. "Cookies, like oatmeal and stuff. Crackers too. They have some other products like breakfast cereal. But I'm excited about the vegan stuff because it tastes good. For real!"

"You've tasted it?" Mel looked dubious.

"I have! I would never push something I hadn't tried myself!"

Mel laughed. "That is cool. I wouldn't mind trying it, so much of that health food is just so expensive."

"This brand is priced very competitively on the market," I said. "Anyway, I don't want to sell you on it, I just wanted to say, I really believe in it."

Talking about it made me realize I was glad I hadn't resigned. I wanted to go back on Monday and see if he'd give me the interns he'd promised.

Mel and I started talking about the Instagram accounts we followed. I hadn't had much time to post on my channel and decided I would get back into it. We ordered another bottle of wine, after which Mel confided in me about her personal life.

"I haven't been out on a date, in like, years." She looked quite despondent. "I sometimes feel like it's never going to happen."

"What about Jamian? I thought you two had gotten together?"

"We hooked up once, but I don't know. He didn't seem that interested afterwards."

Mel was attractive and bright, with a lively personality. I couldn't imagine that she struggled to find a boyfriend.

"You wouldn't believe how many losers are out there," she told me. "Guys living with their parents, not having jobs, smoking weed all day and playing videogames and thinking that's real."

She rolled her eyes.

I thought of Dax and his dreams of making it big in the music business, working the occasional shift as a bar man to make enough money to get by, living in his parents' basement. Then there was Matthew, but I wouldn't even allow myself to think of him.

He was certainly not boyfriend material.

Even though he was so handsome and successful. With a fantastic job and more money than he knew what to spend it on. Of course, he was still living with his mother. And he was an asshole, I had to remind myself. The kind of guy who dumped me for no good reason, or the first thing that popped into his head. Massive trust issues. Huge emotional baggage, like bags and bags of commitment phobia and separation anxiety and who knew what else. The kind of guy who would try to break a girl he once supposedly cared about by throwing insane amounts of work at her, seeing if he could crush her spirit. He was the kind of guy who'd make therapists very rich and happy, I was sure of it.

What was I thinking? But I knew what I was thinking. I was thinking of his naked body, the way he'd tasted of cinnamon and sugar when I'd kissed him, the delicious feeling of his hands running down my sides, feeling every contour, caressing every crook and indentation on my body. The way that man touched my body, making it come alive in ways that made my skin tingle just thinking about it.

"Earth to Lauren!" Mel called out to me, snapping her fingers in front of my eyes.

I laughed and shook my head.

"What were you thinking about?"

"My mom's got this new boyfriend," I said, leaning forwards, slightly tipsy, "And he's really hot!"

"What??" Mel squealed, delighted.

I was exaggerating of course, but I wanted to distract myself, and Mel. I'd met Vic briefly that morning when he came to pick up my mother for a visit to the market. She'd said very little to me about him, but I could tell by her skittish behavior that she was into him.

"He's got this bushy moustache."

"Oh, no, I hate moustaches," giggled Mel.

"It really suits him," I laughed, insisting on trying to convince Mel.

It also helped to get my mind off Matthew. By the time we headed home, I had laughed enough and had enough wine not to care about Dax or Matthew. I just wanted to go home and crawl into bed. Alone.

Chapter 10

Matthew

"I've been thinking," Taya said.

"Yes?"

"Maybe getting married isn't a bad idea." Her voice was non-committal, casual, as if we were talking about our plans for the day, not the rest of our lives.

"What?"

We were standing next to the swimming pool at an East Hampton's mansion. The sun was out, and it was a lovely day for a party, even if it was a little girl's seventh birthday party and most of the guests were adults from the father's social circle. It was Eric Dalton's third marriage and at the age of 66, he seemed to be taking a bigger interest in the child from this marriage than his other children. I had spotted Sharon, his daughter from his second marriage, as well as his son Gregory, who was working for him in the family real estate business. We'd been invited to spend the weekend and my mother had come out for the party as well. She'd rented a house for us for the weekend, as she didn't like to stay in other people's houses. My mother was particular like that, but in this instance, I tended to agree with her. I liked Eric but I couldn't imagine spending a whole weekend with him and his family. I had been looking forward to the weekend away from the city, but Taya's words spoiled the mood. Instantly.

She turned to me and smiled.

"I don't know, it just doesn't seem like such a big deal to me."

I was stunned. When I had told Taya about the conversation I'd had with my mother earlier in the week, she had been as thrown as I was by the news that our parents were plotting out our future together behind our backs. Her family must have gotten to her, I thought.

"Who talked to you? Your mom? Your dad?"

Taya ignored me. She continued in the same light, breezy tone while looking at the pool where little boys and girls were playing with inflatable toys, shrieking with laughter.

"We already get on well, our families like each other. Seems like it could work."

"Except for one small matter," I said pointedly.

Taya glanced briefly at me, a calculating glint in her eyes.

She knew what I meant.

"Come on," she said, in a low voice. "That's hardly a deal breaker."

I saw her put on a big smile and go towards Kristina, Eric Dalton's current wife who was filling up the snacks on the table near the pool. Tottering around on impossibly high heels, I was sure she would slip and fall on the wet tiles surrounding the pool. I recalled she was from somewhere in Eastern Europe, perhaps Poland, and was at least forty years younger than her husband. I watched as Taya made conversation with the woman, the two of them laughing and getting on effortlessly. I knew Taya had a lot of good qualities, but she was so controlled, so cool. And then there was another thing.

Sex.

She said it was hardly a deal breaker.

Except for me, it was.

I had once found the vibrator in her bedroom cabinet and confronted her about it. She was not embarrassed about it at all. She simply didn't enjoy sex with men, she said. She'd tried it once when she was younger, but the encounter had disgusted her. The closeness of another man, lying sweating and grunting on top of her, touching her in ways she found invasive and annoying. Being pawed at, she said, her lips curling contemptuously.

She preferred not to, thank you very much.

Whenever we spent the night together, which was not often, I had observed the intricate rituals she went through before she went to bed. The way she cleansed her skin and treated it with various potions, how she removed hair and treated the smallest blemish with expensive creams and lotions. Before she went out every morning there was another routine of doing her hair, examining her wardrobe, measuring her body to see where she was bloating or retaining water. Once, during a weekend away in Napa, she had insisted on doing a juice cleanse because her skin tone was worrying her. She wouldn't go to dinner even though we'd been invited by friends. I had to say she was ill when really, she was sipping lemon water upstairs in the hotel room and googling some ancient leech therapy that someone had said helped melt away fat. What fat, I wanted to ask. Taya's body was barely human.

Lauren's body, on the other hand, was all woman.

I couldn't help myself; my thoughts wouldn't stop going back to our encounter in my office. The most thrilling Friday afternoon I'd ever had. I thought of all the salespeople who'd sat on that couch where we had torn off our clothes, overcome by lust.

I thought of how she had come striding into my office, ready to pick a fight with me over work. Her flushed cheeks and angry lift of the chin as she was getting ready to take me on. It was adorable. Then, when we'd had sex, she'd been completely unselfconscious about her body and about giving me pleasure. I went hard just thinking about her mouth on my cock, the way her tongue had teased me. With Lauren, there was no issue about the physical nature of sex. She liked her body, and she knew how to use it. She couldn't have been more different from Taya. More human, more fun to be with.

And the sex in my office, well, it had been fantastic.

All that talking about the past and how we used to be together, recalling the connection we'd once had and maybe, still had. The incident that had led to us breaking up at the party at the lake house had somehow vanished. For a moment, we forgot all about that. It was so long ago; it was almost as if it didn't matter at all. But it did matter. A lot. And of course, Lauren was lying to me, just like she was lying back then.

"Penny for your thoughts?" It was my mother, coming to talk to me.

I smiled at her.

No way was I going to share what was going on in my mind.

"Nice party," I said.

She nodded, "I think I'll head over to our place soon."

I wasn't surprised to hear it. My mother never stayed long at events like this, showing her face, exchanging a bit of conversation before fading into the background.

"Mother?" I suddenly asked.

"Yes?" She turned around.

"I was wondering... about you and Father?"

"Oh?"

"You met at a dinner party, right?"

She was thrown a bit by my question. "Yes... my father was an investor, and he invited your father and his brother Albert to come round for dinner. To talk more about their new company. Egal," she laughed. "A combination of Egbert and Albert, what an idea!"

"And?"

"Your father told him that health food was the future, but he couldn't see it, he was loathe to put his money into such a risky venture," she smiled in memory. "He said Americans liked their junk food too much."

"And then you convinced him?"

She nodded. "I did. After dinner, I told him that I thought the Waterstone brothers were onto something and that I had tasted one of their cookies not knowing it was supposedly health food and had loved it all the same. He said if I was prepared to vouch for them, it was good enough for him."

"And that was the tag line, wasn't it?"

"'Too good to be health food.'"

My mother touched my arm. "What's this about, Matthew?"

I decided to jump right in. "You and Father, you loved each other."

Her voice was soft. "Yes, we did, very much."

"Thing is, Taya and I don't love each other."

I saw her face harden.

"But you like each other?"

I nodded.

"That's all you need. Don't you see? Passion and romance die sooner or later in all marriages. But if that goes and there is no companionship, then you have nothing. You and Taya like each other, you share the same background, have the same values. You have the most important aspects of a happy marriage already in place."

I did not think this was true.

"You didn't think your father never stepped out of the marriage, did you?" She gave me a strange, knowing look before walking away. I watched her cross the closely mowed lawn, which stretched into the distance towards the ocean. It was such a handsome property, I thought, but I couldn't appreciate it. I should've told Taya I was leaving but I couldn't face her quite at that moment.

I decided to get an Uber.

I sent Taya a message to say I wasn't feeling well and was leaving.

Standing outside, waiting for my ride, I heard the gravel crunching and saw my mother coming out to meet me.

"Leaving already?" she asked.

I turned away, not answering her.

"I think I'll come with you," she said, hooking an arm through mine. It was probably intended as a gesture of affection but instead it felt as if she was claiming me, chaining me to her body. Her son, her family, her name.

When the car arrived, I didn't want to get into it with her and told her I would stay a little longer, lying to her. I wanted to get another car, maybe go for a drink in town, preferably at a hotel in town where nobody knew me and none of the faces were altered by plastic surgeons or make-up.

I wondered how Lauren would have reacted to this party, how she would have acted with Eric and Kristina. I couldn't imagine her in this world, which was carefully constructed of so many layers of intricate norms and social rules. I couldn't imagine a conversation between her, and my mother and I couldn't really figure out why that bothered me.

I booked a ride into town and found a hotel where I sat at the bar and drank one whiskey after another. I ignored text messages from Taya asking me where I was. There was no way I was marrying her, I thought. Taya was another version of my mother, a manipulator who had her own agenda and was trying to get me to do what she wanted. But I had spent enough time in my life dancing to the tune of others.

I went to reception and took a room for the night.

Then I opened a bottle of wine from the bar fridge and started to drink seriously. My last coherent thought was of Lauren and the way she had felt when I was inside of her. Warm, welcoming. She'd been in the moment, with me, every step of the way. It had felt good. I had felt alive for the first time in ages. No longer going through the motions, doing what was expected of me. Thinking of her made me want her, want to be inside of her again. I could think of nothing else for the rest of the night.

Chapter 11

Lauren

When I woke up on Sunday morning, I was shivering. The weather was changing, and I'd left the window open during the night. I pulled a sweater on and went into the kitchen. My mother was making pancakes. She looked up as I came into the kitchen, smiling at me. I sat down at the kitchen counter on one of the stools. She was cooking on the stove next to the counter.

"Hungry?"

"Always," I grinned at her.

Sunday mornings were a special time for us, we were usually both at home at the same time, at least for a few hours. We would have breakfast, drink coffee and talk. My mother seemed quiet and pensive. I knew her well enough by now and I thought it might have something to do with Vic. I had not seen him during the past week, and she had not gone out much.

"Did you see Vic last night?" I asked casually.

"No, I went with Marianne to one of her salsa evenings," my mother said, giving nothing away.

I nodded. I had gone to the movies with another friend, and I'd come back late, going straight to bed.

"Actually, I haven't heard from Vic in over a week," she then said.

"Oh?"

She shrugged.

"Why haven't you called him?"

She shook her head. "He's probably busy... or something."

"You should call him; hear how he's doing?"

"Not my style," she said. My mother had always believed that women shouldn't go chasing after men. It seemed like a very old-fashioned idea for a modern woman to have.

"But you're thinking about him. You could just call? It doesn't mean you're mad about him or anything."

She looked up and I saw that her face was drawn. There were dark circles under her eyes. For the first time, I could see that she had been taking strain. This guy was getting to her. I leaned forward.

"You're not in high school anymore, mom! Call him, just talk to him!"

"Maybe you're right," she said, putting down the spatula.

She sighed. "I'm all over the place with this guy, I don't know what I should and shouldn't do." I couldn't recall the last time I'd heard her so conflicted about a man.

"What happened the last time you saw him? Did you have a fight?"

She shook her head. "It was a nice evening, we went out to dinner and afterwards, we went to his place. Had a few drinks, listened to music. He told me about his ex-wife, his kids. That sort of thing. I spent the night, it was good."

She pushed a plate with pancakes towards me.

"I had coffee the next morning and came home, there was no weirdness, nothing."

I mulled this over, got some syrup from the cupboard and ate a pancake.

"The thing is, it's been a while, since Hank, you know." My mother was not finding it easy to talk about this, but I could see she wanted to. It was as if she needed to get it off her chest.

"I liked Hank," I said, encouragingly.

"I did too, that was just it," she looked at me with a sad smile. "I got spooked by all his talk of the future and living together. It freaked me out. I needed time apart."

She admitted, "But I thought he'd come back." She gave me a frank look. "After a few weeks, I figured he'd call me and we'd talk and you know, we'd get back together again."

"But he never called."

"Yeah." She took a pancake and placed it on a plate and looked at it, seemed to lose her appetite.

"You don't want to scare Vic away," I said, and I could see that I was right, even though she didn't want to admit it.

"Call him," I said again, more firmly. "Just to talk, hear how he is, see if he says something. If he doesn't, no harm done. You didn't put yourself out there, nothing like that, you just made a call, to chat, you can do that, right?"

She stood up straight, suddenly.

"You're right, I can just call him to talk!"

She smiled. "How did you get so wise about all of this stuff?"

I had to laugh. "As if! My personal life is a complete mess!"

"Things with Dax?" my mom guessed.

I went to get myself some more coffee. I walked over to our window, which looked out on the street and the old trees growing on the sidewalk. It was my favorite feature of our apartment, the sight of greenery and the tranquility it conveyed. I could sit by the window and watch the birds in the trees, sometimes, there were squirrels too. It was like having a garden. A quiet corner in the middle of one of the busiest cities in the world.

"He called, asking me to go out for coffee one day this week, but I couldn't get away," I said.

"How do you feel about him now?" she asked. "Do you want to get back together with him?"

"Not really."

It was the truth. I didn't want to think about Dax. I had spent all week at work, brooding about what had happened with Matthew in his office on Friday afternoon. I had not seen him since then. It had been over a week, and he had not spoken to me, sent me texts, I had not so much as received a work assignment from him. After all the work he'd been giving me over the past few weeks, it seemed unusual and even strange. I thought he might be away for work.

But then one day, we happened to be in the same elevator on the way down. He'd nodded a greeting at me, but I might have been anyone. Another colleague was in the lift with us, and I thought he probably wanted to be discreet and not talk to me in front of anyone else. But when the elevator stopped on the ground floor, the colleague got out and walked off quickly and it was just the two of us, alone, for several moments. He'd seemed awkward, fidgety, like he didn't know what to say, as if I made him uncomfortable.

I had to get out of there. As I walked off, my heart was beating fast, and I could feel my insides churning with emotion. I didn't know what to make of it. Why was I having these emotions around Matthew? I realized that I'd hoped he would act differently towards me, be nicer, more kind. But I'd forgotten that Matthew wasn't a kind man. He wasn't nice. That wasn't him at all. When it came to feelings, he was all buttoned up. Even back in college, come to think of it, he hardly ever opened up, or talked about what was important to him. I tried to get him to be more comfortable around me and I'd noticed how, after a couple of hours of doing some mindless activity, like going hiking or boating or something, he would all out of the blue, say something meaningful, or revealing. But when I asked him about it, he would clam up and the moment was lost.

He seemed even more guarded now, more cautious around people. As CEO, I suppose he had to be conscious of how he appeared to others, his colleagues, and co-workers. Getting involved with an employee was obviously a bad idea.

That Friday afternoon had been a mistake. But it had happened, a kind of blowing off steam for both of us.

Nothing to be done about it now.

I couldn't believe he thought Gabe and I were sleeping together in college. I thought everyone had known that Gabe was gay, he was always going out with men, getting involved in these dramatic love triangles with plenty of intrigue. One time, he was seeing one of the lecturers from another department. It was a secret affair because the lecturer was married. Gabe really liked him though, and he asked me to help him by making the other guy jealous. There was a party at their house, and I had to go with Gabe, pretend to be really into him, like touching him. At one point, Gabe even kissed me, when he thought this guy was watching. He hadn't talked to me about it beforehand and that annoyed me, I didn't want to kiss Gabe, who knew where his mouth had been! And kissing was intimate, I didn't just kiss anyone. But it was a quick smooch and over in seconds. It certainly was effective as the other guy became agitated and took Gabe outside to have words with him. I didn't know what the poor wife thought about that. I left the party soon after, having played the role Gabe had given me. I saw a lot of Gabe back then. We were both on the tennis team and often went away to matches and tournaments against other colleges. We weren't the top-ranking players on the team, which meant there was less stress on our performance and commitment to the team. Both of us were on the second team and were frequently paired as doubles partners, which meant we had to know each other's game well.

"How are things going with that boss of yours?" my mom suddenly asked, coming up behind me, waking me up from my reverie.

"Oh, better, I guess." I hadn't told her about sleeping with him that night in the office. I wasn't hiding it from her, but I knew she wouldn't approve.

I didn't approve of it either.

But I could move on. I knew sometimes, things happened.

I helped my mother clean up the kitchen and as I opened our bin, I suddenly remembered the night we broke up at the lake party. I had blocked it out, since then, not wanting to think about a night that had brought me so much pain. The things Matthew had said to me had been so hurtful, no one had ever spoken to me like that before. It had happened late at night, long after dark. We were supposed to leave for the party in the afternoon, but the day before, Matthew told me about a test he'd forgotten about. He said he would come later, catch a ride with someone else. It was a big party and there were a lot of us going up to the lake. It would be the last big party before finals, and we were keen for some time off before we knuckled down to study.

Gabe and I drove up with a group of friends. They made a huge bonfire outside, we drank and talked, and I'd gone to lie down at some point. The next thing I knew, Matthew was there, calling out my name in a loud voice. Gabe was next to me, but I couldn't even remember him coming into the room. I had fallen asleep that quickly.

Gabriel had tried talking to Matthew, but he'd ignored him.

"I want to talk to you," he'd said, pointing at me. I got up and we went outside. I was cold and I was barefoot, half-asleep. I was frightened and confused by Matthew's behavior. I had never seen him like this before.

"I thought you weren't like the other girls, like other people," he'd said, his voice shaking. "I thought we had something."

I tried to speak, and he wouldn't let me.

"Don't you think you've done enough?"

I didn't know what he was talking about.

"I shouldn't have come up here. We shouldn't be together."

"What?!"

"People like you and me don't mix. I knew that. But I ignored it and look what happened. It's my own fault. You're trash. Nothing but trash!"

He turned around and walked out of my life.

I felt tears jump into my eyes as I remember how I'd felt when he said that. This was what Matthew thought about me. I looked at our apartment now, my home for the past twenty-three years. It was small and messy, but cozy. It was no mansion, not filled with expensive antiques and ornaments centuries years old. There was a throw over the couch that my mother had crocheted, to hide cigarette burns and chocolate stains. Our floors were wooden, varnished, but there were cracks in them and in places, some of the boards had come loose and we'd learnt to walk around them.

I watched my mother put the dishes in the sink. We were many things, colorful and loud, and we made mistakes. But we were not trash. We were no better or worse than the Waterstones, who might have had more money and opportunity but who didn't know how to treat others or how to love. Not properly, not like we did.

In my books, this meant way more. It was more valuable too and you couldn't put a price on it, either.

I went over to hug my mom.

"Call Vic," I said, and felt her arms tight around me in response.

I kissed her cheek. No more thinking about Matthew. Or Dax for that matter.

I was finished with men for a while.

"I'm going to go shopping," I announced.

"I think I need some boots." "A girl can never have enough boots," my mother grinned at me.

I would not let a man get me down, ever again.

Chapter 12

Matthew

I met Jared McPherson at his house in Malibu. I wasn't pleased about the location for our meeting. It had been set up for his office in the city, but shortly after my plane landed, I got the text to meet him at his house instead. It was an extra drive out to the coast, and I didn't like the change of plans.

"Matthew!" Jared came out to meet me in the driveway of his villa, dressed in shorts and a t-shirt. He looked like he was on vacation instead of having a normal day at the office.

I got out of the car, feeling overdressed in my suit.

"I hope you don't mind meeting here?" he said, with a twinkle in his blue eyes. His face was tanned, and his blonde hair was cropped short. His smile was movie star white. "The weather was simply too awesome for us to be locked away in an office, don't you think?" He didn't wait for my answer but gave me a brotherly slap on the back and led me inside.

The weather was indeed beautiful. The sky was blue and wide open, not a cloud in sight. I thought of the cloudy New York that I had left a few hours ago, already beginning to feel the nip in the air that fall brought. Over here, it was still the middle of summer, it seemed.

Jared led me into his house, and I had to stop to admire the view of the ocean. The house made the most of its breathtaking location with big, glass windows and patio doors opening onto a wide porch overlooking the Pacific Ocean. The décor was minimalistic, with a few items of furniture and bright flashes of color against the walls in the form of abstract art.

Jared had made his fortune in a fitness empire that was comprised of specialized gyms. He'd started out as a personal trainer decades ago and his charm and physical abilities had quickly won him a following. He started his own fitness regime, expanding into a chain of gyms that was now nationwide. Each gym had a café, selling a range of healthy food items, including smoothies and various cookies and snacks. We wanted to buy the protein bars and rebrand them under one of our health ranges. Market research had shown that there was interest in similar products and Egal's marketing consultants had been working on a strategy of renaming. We had looked at a few products and I'd had talks with various people over the past few weeks. Jared was open to selling the rights to his protein bar at a good price. As it turned out, it was not his core product and he wanted to focus on expanding his gyms and various health programs.

"What do you say we go hit the surf?" Jared asked, handing me a wet suit.

"I... uhm..."

"We can talk while we catch some waves!" Jared said, flashing me another one of his toothy grins.

"I don't actually surf," I said, sounding a bit silly, even to myself.

"Of course, you don't, city boy you!" He winked at me. "The waves are flat today, so let's just paddle out and get a feel for it."

I had little choice in the matter. I had to put on the wet suit and follow Jared out to the beach directly below his house. He handed me a surfboard and I watched him tuck it under his arm and did the same. Then we walked down the boardwalk to the sea.

He dumped the towels on the beach and sat down. I sat down next to him. We sat in silence for a while, looking at the waves crashing onto the wet sand, the seagulls soaring overhead. It was a magnificent day, and it was hard to stay mad at him for changing our meeting. I leaned back on my elbows.

"This is really impressive," I said, looking at Jared. "How long have you lived here?"

"Six years," he said, looking straight at the ocean. "After Patti and I got married, we found this place and made it our home."

I had read about his wife, a former kickboxing teacher, who was now part of his fitness empire and helped run the business. She seemed like a typical Californian girl, thin and blonde, the picture of good health.

"No kids?"

"Not yet, we'll get there. I'm in no rush though," Jared said. I sensed there was more behind the words. I had met Jared at a business conference years ago and had liked his direct approach to business. When I had to decide whom to approach about the protein bars, the MC Gym group was one of my first choices. Fortunately, my call had come at the right time and Jared had liked my approach.

"She wants 'em, the kiddies," he then said, obviously meaning his wife. "I don't. It's causing a bit of stress as you can imagine."

"Sure."

"But you know, we're in such a good place now. Business going well, life is good. Going on vacation twice a year, hop over to the Caribbean whenever we feel like it. No soccer practice or piano lessons to cramp your style."

He gave me a sideways glance. "My brother never stops complaining about his lack of sleep, the kids yelling and messing up the house, the lack of sex with his wife, who is always tired and crabby. Doesn't exactly sound appealing."

"No."

"Of course, they have twins, and he did leave it quite late."

Jared got up to go surfing after all.

He asked me, "You want kids?"

I didn't know what to say. "I... haven't thought much about it."

That much was true. I had not thought about having my own family or getting married. The whole business with Taya and my mother had been the first time anyone had talked about me settling down. After the weekend in the Hamptons, I had told Taya that I wanted to take a break from our relationship. She asked if I was ending it and I said I wanted some space to think about everything. She was clever enough to know what I was getting at. There were no fights, no arguments.

"If that's what you want," she said, her voice devoid of any emotion, before she hung up.

I'd wanted to nip all wedding talk in the bud, fast. Over the past two weeks, I'd been enjoying the single life and had made sure to spend as little time as possible in the house to minimize the chance of bumping into my mother. I wasn't in the mood for one of her talks.

"You're young, though," Jared said. "I got married in my late thirties." He seemed to consider. "Maybe that's the problem? I'm too settled in my ways?"

"I think it's good to know who you are," I said. "And what you want. Children aren't for everyone. The picket fence and the Labrador and meatloaf on Thursdays?"

Jared laughed. "Exactly!"

Then he said, "Listen, I'm happy to go ahead with the deal. Have your people draw up the papers and we can get it signed and approved."

"You're happy with the price?" I hadn't expected him to agree so quickly. I'd been prepared to offer him more too. On the phone he'd sounded less amenable to my terms but sitting with him now, his whole attitude was more relaxed.

"It's not about the money," he said. "I couldn't care less about that. I like the idea that the product is going to go out under an Egal branding."

"Really?"

He nodded. He told me that the protein bar was created by a local guy who had died of a heart attack a few years back. His wife had kept the business going and Jared had kept renewing the deal with her to support her. "There is a lot you could do to promote those protein bars better. But I have too much on my plate right now. Besides, I like how you've revamped the Egal health range. There have been some really cool videos promoting the brand lately, Patti showed one to me last week, I was laughing my butt off!"

This was Lauren's work, I realized. She had been posting videos and doing all kinds of funky stuff to promote the vegan products. I knew which product line he was talking about.

"That's our new community manager," I said. "She's young and switched on, knows her stuff."

"Can't wait to see what she comes up with for these protein bars!" he said, jumping up and grabbing his board. "I'm going to test the water, you coming?"

I said I'd wait for him out on the beach, and he was happy with that.

I watched him on the water for a while, but as he had pointed out, the surf was flat and there weren't any good waves around. It was a glorious afternoon, and I didn't mind sitting out there, closing my eyes, and listening to the water washing onto the shore. He came out soon enough and we went up to the house for lunch. Someone had laid out platters of sushi and we had a delicious meal and some beers before I headed back to the airport.

We shook hands before I left, and he pulled me into a hug when we said goodbye.

"You take care, man," he said to me, and I awkwardly slapped his back to show affection. It had been a good afternoon and we'd had a productive outcome to our discussion, but I've never been a physically demonstrative sort of a person. I also didn't have that many friends that I could talk to or relax with. I wasn't that comfortable around people or sharing my thoughts so openly. I had a feeling Jared had a huge circle of friends.

He had gotten a car to take me back to the airport and I felt an odd regret to be leaving the sunshine and the warm weather behind. New York was beginning to be overcast and glum and the days had recently been chilly. It occurred to me that I could stay a bit longer in the city, but when I checked my calendar, I saw that I had an early meeting with an important supplier that I had to attend.

I got onto the plane, took my seat, and leaned back, thinking about taking a nap.

I thought of Lauren and how strained it was between us lately. Ever since our escapade in my office, we had not been alone together, apart from one time in the elevator. That had been excruciating for both of us. I had the feeling she wanted me to say something, but I could not wait to get out of there. My thinking around Lauren wasn't clear, I had come to see. I was so attracted to her, still, that I seemed not to remember that she was lying to me, even now. Maybe that performance in my office had been a well-orchestrated ploy to get me to lighten up on her workload. It had worked, of course, I had found the interns for her, and her workload must have become much lighter. I kept out of her way, now though, because I didn't want her getting ideas. I kept seeing her face when she tried to convince me that Gabriel was gay and that she'd never had a thing with him, when she knew very well she was lying. It didn't matter that she knew how to do wonderful things with her tongue or that she was good at her job, she wasn't to be trusted.

Trust was important to me; it was probably the most important thing to me.

If I couldn't trust people, I wanted as little as possible to do with them.

Whenever I thought of that afternoon together, of the way she had opened to me and the delicious pleasure we had shared for a few moments, I told myself that this was all part of a little play she was making for me. I had to be careful. Lauren wasn't the first woman to try to trap me. I only had to think of Taya and her suggestion that getting married wasn't the worst idea in the world.

Lauren was nothing like Taya, though. At least, I didn't think she was.

But perhaps all women were manipulative, scheming and cold, I thought bitterly.

Chapter 13

I went home after lunch, sending Diaz a text that I wasn't feeling well. I went to the drug store first, then headed straight home.

"You okay, honey?" I heard someone calling to me as I came up the stairs to our apartment.

It was Mrs. Penderis from upstairs.

"Yeah," I called up, forcing a smile on my face.

"Just feeling a bit sick."

"Ah, that's too bad, feel better soon."

I went up the stairs to our apartment, passing Doris and her baby who were heading out to the park. I had to make conversation with her too. Finally, I was able to get into our apartment and shut the door behind me.

I closed my eyes in relief.

When I opened them, I found our apartment the same as when I'd left it in the morning. My coat was still on the chair where I'd thrown it earlier, deciding to opt for another jacket. Our breakfast dishes had been placed in the sink but not rinsed out since both of us were late this morning. It was only a few hours ago but already it felt like a lifetime ago.

I went to the bathroom and looked at myself in the mirror. I was looking a bit pale, unwell. I'd been feeling off color for a while, I thought I had a bug. Then, in the office kitchen this morning, the smell of coffee had turned my stomach. I was talking to Petra about some TV show and the next moment I thought I was going to throw up. I ran into the bathroom and retched but the nausea had passed. I came out to wash my face, feeling rather shaky. A woman stood at the basin, washing her hands. She looked at me sympathetically. "Last time I ran like that for the loo, I was pregnant with my second."

"Oh, I'm not pregnant!" I said quickly. Then I got an awful, awful feeling. I mean, I couldn't be, could I?

The woman walked out of the bathroom while I did the math in my head. When was the last time I'd had my period? I needed my phone to check the calendar. I walked back slowly to my desk and got my phone. There was no getting away from it. I was late. By almost a week. I was usually quite regular, but I'd been so caught up with work that I hadn't noticed.

"Are you okay?" Tash stood at my desk. I shook my head and said I was going home. I couldn't face anyone. I had to know. I bought three different tests and at home, I did all three and waited. Those minutes felt like the longest of my life. When I finally checked them, the result was the same on all of them.

It was positive.

I was pregnant.

My legs felt weak, I had to sit down. This wasn't possible? How could it be? I hadn't had sex in ages. I tried to think of the last time I'd had sex and with a shock I realized that it had been Matthew, in his office, over a month ago.

Was that possible?

It had been over so quickly, and I had put the whole incident out of my mind. But, of course, he hadn't used a condom and I knew how human biology worked. I thought of Doris, whom I'd just met on the stairs. She'd had her third child only a few months ago and always looked tired and worn out. She seemed dreadfully unhappy. It didn't help that her husband was unemployed and spent all day glued to the screen, playing videogames.

I tried to think clearly. I had options; I wasn't a teenager. I could go to a doctor, talk about it. But the thought of getting rid of a baby was too horrible. I thought of my mother, getting pregnant at twenty-two and how she'd had me despite everyone telling her to give me away or have an abortion. I was only a year older than she was then, but my situation was not that different. I knew she would be terribly disappointed. She'd always wanted more for me than she'd had and even though she hadn't complained, I could see how difficult it was to raise a child as a single mother. Was I ready for that? I couldn't face the thought of telling Matthew, but it was his child. Didn't he have a right to know? I thought of how weird it had been between us the last few weeks, the way he'd been avoiding me. He clearly wished we'd never slept together.

I waited for my mother to come home from work and then I told her the news.

"Oh, Lauren," my mother rushed towards me, hugging me tightly.

"Are you sure?"

"Three different tests," I smiled wryly.

"Who's the father, Dax?"

I paused. I'd never told my mother about what happened with Matthew. I'd gotten together with Dax a few times in the past two weeks. He'd started contacting me again, pestering me to go out for a drink or for coffee. I finally relented and it had been fine. I could tell he felt bad about what had happened between us. He apologized for messing around with Mandy and swore they hadn't slept together. I wasn't sure that I believed him. We hadn't done anything apart from drinking coffee, though. There was no way it could be him.

"No."

Reluctantly, I told my mother about Matthew and the one time we had sex in his office.

"You never told me that!"

"I know," I said sheepishly. "I was embarrassed. It was such a stupid thing to do."

"Not stupid," she said with a tender smile. "Just spontaneous."

"You're not mad?"

"How could I be mad?" my mother stroked my hair and I burst into tears.

"This wasn't planned at all!"

"Of course, it wasn't! But that's what life is! Life is what happens when you make other plans, remember?"

"John Lennon," I said, remembering one of my mother's favorite quotes. We sat on the couch, and she stroked my hair.

"Have you told him?"

I shook my head.

"You'll have to do it," she said.

"Did you tell my dad? When you were pregnant with me?" I asked, pulling away. My mother's face went blank, she bit her lip. She didn't like talking about my father and had always avoided the topic. I only knew that I had been conceived with someone whom she never saw again.

"That was different," she said, slowly.

"How?"

"He was married," she said, quietly. I was shocked. She'd never told me this before.

"I didn't want you to know," she said, looking down. "But I knew he already had children with someone else. He was older and not someone who could help me with a baby. When you have a child, you need reliable people in your life. He wasn't."

"Who is he?" I demanded to know.

"I will tell you more," she promised. "Just not right now, please, let's deal with this first. You have a lot to think about right now."

I nodded.

She went on, "But it's different with Matthew. He's not married, and you used to be in a relationship. He's got money too, right? He could help?"

I knew she was right. If I was going to have a baby, I needed funds and even with my mother's help, we would struggle. It was his child too after all.

I lay awake all night, thinking about how I would tell Matthew and by the time the sun came up, I felt weak and exhausted. My mother had made breakfast for me and forced me to eat some of it.

"You need your strength," she said, her eyes filled with love and concern.

"Whatever you decide, I will be here, ready to help you," she said. I felt like crying again.

As soon as I got to the office, I went to Matthew's office. His PA said he'd stepped out and I waited for him. I don't know how long I waited but then he walked in, his eyes narrowing.

"Lauren?"

"Do you have a minute to talk?"

"Not really, I'm in the middle of something," he said. His face was closed off to me, he looked at me like I was a stranger.

"Okay," I nodded and walked out, not able to face him like this.

"Wait!" he called after me.

I kept walking to the elevator. It was all too much.

He came after me, grabbing my arm.

"What is it?"

I blurted it out. "I'm pregnant," I said. "It's yours."

The doors of the elevator opened, and I moved towards it.

"What?" he said, his face frozen in shock.

"I wanted to tell you, that's all."

I got into the elevator and pressed the ground floor button. I didn't look back at him. I simply closed the doors and waited to go down. I wasn't going to work now. I couldn't face the thought of sitting at my desk and pretending everything was normal. I took out my phone and texted Diaz that I was going to the doctor today and would be going home.

I walked towards the subway.

"Lauren!"

I turned around and it was Matthew, calling out to me.

"Can we talk?"

"Do you have a minute now?" I said, unable to help myself. "Look, I don't want anything from you, all right?"

"Are you going to keep it?" he asked, his voice strained.

"I don't know," I said.

All around us, people were rushing past us to go to work, to do shopping, to meet up with friends. Nobody paid any attention to us. I was having one of the most important conversations of my life, but it did not matter to anyone but me.

"Surely not!" Panic flashed through his eyes. "I mean, how do you even know it's mine?"

"It's yours, trust me."

"Trust you?!"

The way he'd said that made me take a step back. "What do you mean?"

"You are the last person I'd trust!"

"Why do you say that?"

"After all your lying about Gabriel and your relationship in college! I know you two were together, I saw you. At that party!"

Oh, God, I thought. This again.

"Believe what you want to," I said, too tired for this conversation, and turned to walk away.

"I saw you kissing him!" he said.

"Yes, I kissed him, but it was just to make his boyfriend jealous. Are you for real? You're so full of shit, Matthew Waterstone, seriously! You couldn't just talk to me about this? Gabe and I were just friends, he was the one willing to do stuff with me over the holidays when you had to go away. He took me to the hospital when I had stomach pains and you had to go to some fundraiser gala. He was the one who did my laundry after I got a tennis injury, and you were too busy studying to help me. So special, aren't you! Not like I could trust you exactly either! You know what, I told you about the pregnancy, which was the right thing to do. Now you can go back to your pretend perfect world! I won't bother you again."

I walked off, everything blurry through the tears that were filling my eyes.

But I felt better after telling Matthew exactly what I thought of him and his precious family.

For the first time, I'd let him have a piece of what I'd been thinking for years.

And it felt good.

Chapter 14

Matthew

I was in meetings all day. There was a problem with distribution in Europe and I had to talk to the head of our office in the UK about the hold up in customs. Then there was an issue with a supplier in Michigan. My uncle had asked me to look into a contract with one of our original suppliers. I had sent it to our legal team, but I delayed in looking at the email he sent back. The lawyers often sent very long, wordy messages that took forever to wade through. But I couldn't put off my uncle much longer. As chairman of the board, Albert had considerable power and influence. I suspected he thought he should have been named CEO, but my mother had always been very firm on carrying out the wishes of my father and since these were set out clearly in his will, going against them would entail a legal battle that would be costly and most certainly cause great conflict in the family.

It was late by the time I went home. Traffic was bad, and I found myself gridlocked between the traffic lights. I waited for the cars to move and leaned back, closing my eyes, and taking a deep breath.

In that moment, my thoughts drifted to Lauren and to the conversation we'd had in the morning.

I heard her words again.

There was nowhere for me to go. I couldn't avoid thinking about what she'd said to me anymore.

Strangely enough, it was the last thing she'd said to me that had upset me most. My perfect pretend world.

How did she know?

I had everything. Money, power, a great job, good health, and excellent family connections.

But I wasn't happy.

I hadn't ever been happy.

Back in college, Lauren had already noticed that. She'd once asked me, right in the beginning of our relationship, what I wanted to do for a break that we had between terms. I told her I had to go back to the city to see my mother. She asked if I wanted to go. I told her it wasn't about what I wanted, that this was what was expected of me, and I had to do it. Lauren had given me a mischievous grin and asked me what would happen if I didn't go; if I went with her on whatever adventure she had planned. Wouldn't that make me happy? I'd gotten annoyed with her, snapping at her that she didn't get it, that I wasn't like her and that I had important things I had to do. I couldn't jump in a camper van and head for the hills whenever I felt like it. I told her I couldn't think about what made me happy all the time, that I had other responsibilities.

She had touched on a major weakness, something that had been bothering me for a long time, but I'd not allowed myself to think about. The fact that I was unhappy, that I didn't really care about the family the way my mother wanted me to. Spending time with Lauren in college was the closest I'd come to doing what I wanted. It had nothing to do with my family or my father, it was all about me. I had not told Lauren much about this, I always kept my feelings hidden from her. I didn't want her to know how much she meant to me. Later, when I was taking over as CEO, I booked a few sessions with a business coach, to prepare me for the leadership position in the company. But the coach took me back to my past and my most important relationships, my connections with my parents. She told me that I had essentially grown up as an orphan, with both parents absent. She said I'd never learned to form relationships and had to work on forming proper bonds.

I had disagreed with her, become quite upset.

But I knew she was right.

Deep down, I knew it. The only person I'd ever had any real relationship with, was Lauren. The girls I'd dated, the friends I'd gone out with had never gotten close to me, I'd never let them. But I had let Lauren in. She was the only one who knew the guilt I felt about my father; that I barely remembered him, this man who'd become larger in death than he had been in life. I was ten when he died and even by then, I'd spent very little time with him. He was always working, away on business. There were flashes of memory, a fishing trip one weekend, a Christmas surrounded by snowy trees and a cabin in the woods. My father's smiling face, friendly but vague. Snatches of images that could have come from a film I'd seen. I couldn't miss someone I'd never known. Lauren understood this, never having had a father figure in her life either. But she had a mother, a present mother, someone who had featured strongly in her life, a positive influence.

It had been difficult for me to deal with how much Lauren had meant to me, back in college. The feelings I had for her were deep and had made me feel vulnerable and unsure of myself. I had become used to being on my own and having someone else to share things with me felt wonderful and terrible, at the same time.

I became jealous and suspicious of Lauren and started seeing signs of her cheating on me everywhere. I was convinced she was seeing Gabriel on the side. I watched the two of them on the tennis court, her laughing the way she never laughed with me. Gabriel was handsome in a dark, almost Mediterranean way. He had an easy grace, and I could see that he was attractive to men as well as women. I thought he probably had relationships with both sexes. He seemed open to that, freer, certainly than I was. Lauren had told me early on that they were only friends, but I couldn't really understand that kind of friendship. To spend so much time with someone else, not becoming irritated and needing to be alone, seemed foreign to me. I could not quite believe that there was nothing sexual about their closeness. At the same time, I kept telling myself our relationship couldn't be serious, that it would have to end soon when I graduated anyway.

The traffic started moving slowly and I was relieved to be able to put my foot on the gas and drive a bit. I wanted to get going again, not only in the traffic, but in my life too.

Now Lauren was pregnant.

I knew my reaction to the news had not been good and I regretted it. I had felt put on the spot and I was never at my best in a situation like that. I had implied that I wanted nothing to do with the baby, that I wanted her to get rid of it. But that couldn't have been further from the truth.

I thought of babies and how helpless they were. Cute and playful, needing to be cared for and carried around. In my world, there were people who did that. Childminders and night nurses, au pairs, and nannies. Mothers dressed their babies up in darling outfits to show them off to friends for a few hours over a cup of tea. There was always someone else to clean their bum or find a dry sweater and fix a sandwich for a hungry boy. Mothers planned dinner parties and redecorated conservatories. But Lauren wasn't from my world, she would be a different sort of mother.

My thoughts came back to the baby. My baby.

The idea that I had fathered a child was exciting. I imagined how this child could have a different sort of childhood than I had. This child could have so much love and attention. This baby I could take up to the family cabin, build tree houses with, if it was a boy. If it was a girl, I would get her a pony, teach her to ride. I thought of the things I'd do with the baby, could see myself sitting with the bundle of blankets at night, if he or she woke up screaming in the night and needed comforting.

I felt powerful feelings that I'd never had before. The only babies I had ever come into contact with were the children of two of my cousins. One of my friends had recently become a father, but he barely spoke of it. He was more keen to talk about his new car, an imported Lamborghini from Italy. Telling me how fast it had been able to go on the back roads upstate was all he had to share with me

But fast cars held no attraction for me. A baby, on the other hand, my own too, now that was something to think about.

I called the head of HR and asked for Lauren's home address and her phone number. I planned on calling her later, arranging to see her. I wanted to go home, change my clothes, think of what to say to her.

But when I got home, hours later, my mother was waiting for me at the front door. Her arms were crossed, and her face resolute.

"Could I have a word, Matthew?"

She didn't wait for my answer but walked into the drawing room next to the front door. It was a formal space, used by both of us to entertain or have meetings with lawyers, or in her case, foundation workers or trustees. She sat down on one of the elegant chaises, crossed her legs and folded her hands.

I remained standing, impatient to grab a shower.

"What is it, Mother?"

"I want to talk about your relationship with Taya."

"It's over, I ended it."

"I heard you wanted a break." She was trying to work on me to patch things up with Taya, I thought. But it wouldn't work.

"I don't have time for this, Mother!" I said, unusually impatient with her. "I have something to take care of."

"More important than your future, than this family's future?" she stood up now, her voice rising. I could tell she was getting upset, working herself up to an argument. I wasn't in the mood for it.

"Let's talk about this later, yeah?"

"This isn't about you!" her voice shook with anger. "Getting married is one of the most important steps you will take in your life! It is how this family survives and your father's bloodline continues!"

I continued walking out the door and up the stairs.

Her voice carried on after me, like darts stinging me as I went.

I didn't want to deal with my mother, and I wanted to get away from her as quickly as possible.

My thoughts were filled with Lauren and the baby, visions of the two of us walking with a stroller, the little one chattering away. Or being on the beach somewhere, possibly the Hamptons, my child tottering about on unsteady legs, feeling his or her way on the sand. I saw Lauren and myself, being there, together, united as parents at least.

I didn't know how I felt about Lauren. I had been convinced that she had been cheating on me for so long, but her words to me this afternoon had shattered those notions. They'd shown me how ridiculous I had been. Of course, I should have talked to her. But perhaps it had suited me to use her supposed cheating as an excuse to end the relationship. This way, she was to blame, and I didn't have to take responsibility. It was a cowardly way to act but I knew it was a possibility, that it was probably true. I knew I had to put a stop to our relationship, but I didn't know how. I had felt this was a weakness in me, this inability to cut ties with Lauren, knowing that our relationship couldn't continue once I was back in the city. I used a supposed betrayal to punish her by breaking up with her. It was a tactic worthy of my mother. I recognized that this was how she operated. I had seen her deal with people whom she thought had slighted her. There was never a direct confrontation. She preferred some twisted plan to get back at someone. For instance, someone who had not invited her to a society brunch would have to deal with unpleasant rumors about their family later, without knowing where they came from.

I didn't like these thoughts. They made me feel ill.

I knew I still had feelings for Lauren.

Feelings, which now, were more complicated than ever.

She would be the mother of my baby.

My baby. I caught myself smiling every time I thought the words.

I knew I had to talk to Lauren.

Chapter 15

Lauren

I went home and got straight into bed, sleeping for several hours straight.

When I woke up, I felt disorientated and a bit out of sorts.

Then I heard the knocking on the door.

I pushed myself out of bed. It was after six and normally my mother would have been home already. I opened the door to a rather disheveled-looking Doris from next-door.

"Oh," she said. "I was expecting your mother."

"She's not back yet," I looked over my shoulder in case I'd missed her sitting in the kitchen, but our place was as empty as it had been when I'd gotten home. My mother had a way of making her presence known, whether it was by leaving shopping on the counters or kicking off her shoes in the middle of the room.

"It's just... ah... never mind," she turned to go back to her place.

"Can I help?"

Doris turned back, a desperate look in her eyes. "I was hoping she could babysit Shay for a bit? I need to go see my mom in Harlem, she's not feeling well and I need to check up on her. I didn't know who else to call, usually Phil can do it but I'm not sure where the fucker's gone off to this time, he hasn't been home since yesterday."

"I can help," I said.

"Really?" Her whole face lit up. "You'd have to come to ours, I'm afraid. Make sure the others get dinner and do their homework. You sure you don't mind?"

"Let me just grab a sweater," I said. I left a note for my mom and followed Doris to her place, a few doors down.

Doris had two older children, a boy named Mickey who was seven and another daughter Angelica, who was nine. I had seen them run past me on the stairs. The baby was eight months old. Doris pointed out bottles of milk in the fridge, warned me about a pot of pasta boiling on the stove and then she shoved the baby in my arms and was out the door.

She must've still been in the building when the baby started wailing. I had no idea what to do. The older kids sat in front of the TV, oblivious to the baby's cries. Doris said she had just been fed and wouldn't be hungry. I tried to change the little one on the bed in the main bedroom and struggled to get her to lie still enough for me to get the clean diaper on her. By the time I was finished, I was bathed in sweat and feeling quite nauseous.

The apartment, which was like ours in size, was a complete mess. There were clothes strewn all over the furniture and papers littered every surface. Some were bills and old magazines, others were drawings made by the kids. Toys and stuffed animals competed with hockey sticks and soccer balls. Empty candy wrappers and bread crusts were stuffed into the sides of the sofa.

"Have you guys finished your homework?" I asked the older kids, who gave me blank stares and went back to watching their series. Meanwhile, the baby continued to cry. I tried everything to get her to calm down and after a while, started to think that it had to be me. She didn't want to be rocked or sung to. I was out of options and beginning to be quite freaked out when Angelica gave me a bored glance and suggested I bathe her.

In the bathroom, I found a small plastic tub, and I filled this with warm water. As soon as I sat her down in the tub, she stopped crying and stared in fascination at the bubbles and the small toys. I had only been there for about half an hour, and I already felt exhausted.

Who was I kidding? I couldn't look after a baby on my own!

While Angelica watched the baby, I grated some cheese over the boiled macaroni and sliced apples for the older children's dinner. Then while they ate, I finished bathing the baby, dressing her snugly in warm pajamas, and put her down in her crib in the main bedroom. Within minutes she'd started crying again though, and I had to pick her up and try to rock her to sleep.

My mother came over a bit later and started laughing when she saw me with the baby.

"It's not funny!" I cried out. "She hates me! She's been like this since I got here!"

"Where's Doris?"

I told her the story and my mother took the baby from me.

"There, there," she soothed the little one, sitting down with her on the couch, letting the baby rest comfortably in her arms. She settled down right away, her eyelids drooping and finally closing.

"How did you do that?" I asked, astonished.

"Lots of practice!" my mother smiled at me.

I shook my head and closed my eyes. "I don't think I can do this on my own," I said softly to my mom. "It's too hard."

"Did you talk to Matthew?"

I told her about our conversation and how I would have to go it alone if I kept the baby.

"I made an appointment with a doctor for tomorrow morning," I said. "I'll see what he says. Maybe, I don't know. I mean, how do I do this on my own?"

"It's hard," my mother admitted. "Especially in the beginning when they're so small. I was alone back then, as you know, my mother and I weren't talking. One of my friends, Yasmin, you know her? She came to stay with me for a bit, that helped a lot. It was before she got married and had her own kids."

"But I didn't have a career," my mother went on. "I gave up working, I was basically at home with you for that first year. Until my money ran out and I had to swallow my pride and talk to my mother. Then things improved. Childcare is expensive. Does Egal have a crèche or something?"

I didn't know.

But I didn't think I could keep on working there one way or another. I would have to find another job.

"I don't know what to do," I whispered to my mom.

"We'll figure it out," she said.

She got up carefully to put down the baby and I convinced the older kids to get ready for bed. Then I cleaned up the apartment. My mother helped me. We waited for Doris to come back. It was after ten when she finally came through the door, and I was delighted to see her. I'd started having nightmare visions where she simply didn't return, and I was stuck with her children for the rest of my life. They were nice enough, but I could see how I'd barely have time to wipe my nose with all the cleaning, cooking, and tidying I'd have to do. I wasn't ready for any of that.

By the time I made it back to our place, I wanted only to get into my bed.

I didn't want to see Matthew ever again.

So, imagine my surprise when I got up the next morning, stumbled to the kitchen to find some coffee and saw Matthew sitting at the kitchen counter, chatting amicably with my mother.

"What the..." I couldn't finish the sentence. I was wearing a big T-shirt that barely covered my bits and my hair was a complete disaster. Matthew, on the other hand, had a freshly ironed shirt and smart jeans on.

"I came last night but you weren't here," he said, jumping up as soon as he saw me. "So, I came back this morning, before you went to work."

"I'm not going to work," I said.

"Why?"

I shrugged. I didn't feel like talking to Matthew. My mother went into her room and closed the door so we could talk. I heard her put on some music to give us privacy.

"Why are you here?" I asked. "How did you even get my address?"

"I've been thinking. A lot, since I saw you yesterday," he said. "I know I didn't react well. The news about the baby was... not what I was expecting."

I rolled my eyes.

"Really? Because this was just what I was expecting to happen."

I poured myself coffee.

"I want you to know that you're not alone in this decision."

"Oh?"

"If you want to keep it, I'll help you. If you don't, I guess that's fine too. But... I wish you would decide to keep it.

"You do? But yesterday... "

He interrupted me. "Yesterday, I was in shock. I didn't have time to think."

"And now you have had time to think?"

"Yes."

"What does that mean?"

"It means... I want to help you with this. I want to be involved and support you."

"Seriously? You've had a complete change of heart since yesterday? Like twenty-four hours ago?"

"What you said... I've been thinking about it. And you're right. I was... I am... full of shit."

I stared at him open-mouthed. I couldn't believe what I was hearing.

"I've got a lot of stuff to deal with, but right now, I want to make the right decision. This is a baby. Yours and mine, right?"

I went to sit down. This was all too much.

He seemed sincere.

But it was confusing after yesterday when he had been so hostile to me, so mean.

"What about all that crap you said, about not trusting me?"

Matthew sat down in the chair across from me. He looked down and thought carefully before he said,

"It's not true. I do trust you. You're the only person I have ever trusted in my entire life, I think."

I could not believe my ears.

"I think that's why I was so mean to you, back in college, even yesterday. I'm not sure, but I truly am sorry for the things I said, back in college as well as after that. And for how I've treated you since you've come to work at Egal. The truth is, I was happy you were there and liked having you close by. I know it may not have looked like it, but I was."

I had never heard Matthew talk so openly and freely about his feelings.

"I'm... going to need a moment..." I said and started laughing. He laughed with me, nervously.

I told him about babysitting Doris's baby and how overwhelming it was.

"But you would have help. If you wanted, you could have night nurses. Nannies. Childcare during the day."

My mouth dropped open, I had to shut it again.

He laughed and shook his head. "I know it sounds crazy," he said. "But since I've started thinking about the baby, I can't stop."

"I was going to go to the doctor today to see how far I am and get an idea of options."

He stared at me. "Options?"

"It's a big responsibility, Matthew," I said in a shaky voice. "I don't know if I can do it. What if you decide in six months' time you don't want to see me again?"

"We can set up a trust in the baby's name," he said, right away, as if he'd thought about it. "That way it has nothing to do with the two of us."

His face changed when he spoke about the baby, I saw a side of him that I'd never seen before. I wanted to believe this change of heart was real, but I wasn't ready to trust him again.

Not yet.

I told him he could come to the clinic with me. He cancelled his morning meetings and took me to the doctor in his car. There, a nice lady in a white coat confirmed that I was pregnant, and we heard the baby's heartbeat on the sonar. After that, I knew there was no way I could turn my back on my baby.

I may not have known how to be a mother, but I would not give up before I had even tried.

Chapter 16

Matthew

The Parkinson's Benefit Gala evening was an annual event held at the Plaza Hotel. It was one of the highlights of the social calendar, for my mother, at least. She was on the steering committee and helped plan the night. I usually tried to get out of going to the thing, but tonight, I had a plan. I was going to tell my mother about Lauren's pregnancy at the dinner, when she was surrounded by people and wouldn't be able to cause a scene.

Or so I hoped.

It had been four weeks since Lauren had told me about the baby. We had decided, for the time being, not to tell anyone the news until we were certain everything with the pregnancy was going well. She would continue coming to work every day and I started checking in on her daily, to see how she was doing. The messages were brief, to the point and often, she simply sent a thumbs up. Then, over the first weekend, I asked if she wanted to go to breakfast. I picked her up and we went to a café near their apartment, nothing fancy. We talked a bit about the future. Lauren said she wanted to keep working but would take maternity leave. I said I'd pay for a nanny once she came back to work. After breakfast, we went for a stroll around the shops, looking at baby clothes and strollers and seeing what was out there.

The doctor had told us the first twelve weeks were the most critical in the pregnancy, when miscarriages were common. Lauren said she didn't want to buy anything until we were sure. The whole pregnancy thing was still very new for both of us.

But it wasn't all that was new.

It was different with us. Between us. A kind of shyness or caution. It was like we didn't know how to act. We'd been together years ago and then we were exes. But what were we now? Friends? We were breaking new ground when it came to our relationship, and it was confusing for both of us. One evening, after a Chinese dinner, I took her back to her apartment and when I came up, there was a moment when I wanted to kiss her but wasn't sure if it was a good idea. In the end, I leaned forward and kissed her briefly, holding her lips for a moment before pulling away.

"That was very chaste!" she'd said with a laugh and any tension between us melted away. As I drove home, I got the feeling that she might be open to us getting back together again. I found the idea didn't sit badly with me either.

I walked through our house at home, trying to imagine bringing a baby here. There were so many empty rooms here, spare bedrooms that nobody ever used. As long as I could remember, the house had been dark and silent, the kind of place that seemed to be filled with ghosts and memories.

We went for a drive the previous weekend, having lunch in a small town outside the city, talking and joking about work and people we knew at the office. Afterwards, we walked a bit and looked at the trees and the fall colors that were beginning to light up the landscape. I suggested we spend the night at a local hotel and when she hesitated, I told her we would get two rooms, of course. She agreed and I found a charming inn surrounded by big oak trees. There was a dining room where the owner offered us a hearty stew and Lauren permitted herself one glass of wine before we went to the sitting room where a roaring log fire invited us to linger before going to bed. I asked how she was feeling, and I could see Lauren pausing to answer. Her face was glowing in the soft light of the fire, and I thought that the pregnancy was agreeing with her. She had not gained much weight yet, mostly because she wasn't eating that much due to the nausea.

"I've been wondering," she said. "About us."

"Yes?"

I didn't know what to say.

"What is this?" she motioned to me and her. "I mean, what's going on? Something is going on, right?"

"I don't know," I said truthfully.

"Do you take all your employees to New England for the weekend?" she asked with a half-smile. But her eyes were serious.

"Only the special ones," I said.

She bit her lip, and I could see she needed more of an answer.

"I think something is going on," I said slowly. "But I'm not sure what it is. How would you feel about it if something was happening?"

"You dumped me once before, Matthew," she said, after a while. "You accused me of cheating on you, then you told me you didn't trust me. I like you, all right. It may be the hormones, or whatever. And we're having a baby together, it seems. But your track record isn't great. When it comes to relationship material, I'm not sure this is a good idea."

It wasn't easy to hear. But I knew these were things that had to be said. Communicating about emotions was not a strong suit for me. I didn't like hearing her talking about me this way, but I couldn't deny that she was being honest. We weren't kids anymore, fooling around in college. There was a baby coming and we needed to be sure.

"You're right," I said. "But I want us to try again, and I will try to do better."

She looked into my eyes, her blue eyes drawing me to her, I wanted to plunge into them and take my chances.

"We can take it slowly, see what happens, how it feels. What do you think?"

She bit her lip, unsure.

"I don't know."

I kissed her quickly, before she could say anything else. Her face was warm from the fire and her mouth responded to me, her lips opening and inviting, and I gently traced the outline of her lips with my tongue, before taking her face in my hands, my desire building. She kissed me back and our kiss grew more passionate, deeper.

She pulled back and blinked. "Woah!"

"I'm sorry," I said quickly, not wanting to scare her off. "I am getting ahead of myself, I think. I know I was a prick, Lauren, when I broke things off with you. Then, again, when you started at Egal. But I've never stopped caring about you. Since you started working at the company, you were constantly in my thoughts. I couldn't stop thinking about you."

"Even in the board meetings?" a slow smile curled around her lips.

"Especially then."

She smiled at me.

"Let's see how it goes," she said, her voice sweet. "Right now, baby needs to get some sleep."

We walked up to our separate rooms, and I thought about her all night long.

As we drove back the next day, holding hands in the car like teenage sweethearts, I told her that I would have to tell my mother about the baby. She looked concerned. She knew my mother was not supportive like her mother and I'd told her enough about my background to know that my mother could make life hard for us.

"How do you think she'll react?" she asked, anxiously.

"She wants me to marry some other woman," I said. I filled Lauren briefly in on the situation with Taya.

I glanced over at Lauren and saw her face had gone white.

"Look, I'm sure she won't be pleased at first, but she'll have to come around eventually."

"What if that never happens?"

"It has to, if she wants to get to know her grandchild and I'm pretty sure she will want to do that."

I was sounding more confident than I felt.

At the night of the benefit gala, my mother sat next to me at the dinner table. She'd tried to convince me to bring Taya and we'd had a fight when I told her I was not doing that. As a result, there was an empty seat on my other side as she'd bought the ticket months in advance already. I waited for the speaker of the event and the master of ceremonies to do their bit, downing a few extra glasses of champagne to give me courage.

My mother noticed.

"You're drinking rather a lot tonight?"

"I need to tell you something?"

She put down her fork. "Oh?"

"An ex-girlfriend of mine is having my baby."

Her face froze and I waited for her to say something. But instead, her faced arranged itself into an awful smile.

"What?" her voice was low. I repeated what I said.

"An ex-girlfriend? Who?"

I explained to her about seeing Lauren in college and how she came to work for me and said we'd started seeing each other again.

"Who is this girl?" she hissed, her voice shaking. "What does her family do?"

"It's not a family we know," I said. "Her mother is a teacher. She doesn't know who her father is." It didn't sound well, even to me. But I didn't care how it sounded. I cared about Lauren and the baby.

My mother dabbed a serviette to her mouth, pushed her plate away.

"We will talk about this at home."

"No," I said.

She blinked a few times. "What do you mean, no?"

"There is nothing to talk about," I said, firmly. "She is having my baby and I'm supporting her. You don't have to approve of it, you don't have to like it, but I'm afraid that it is happening, one way or another."

She glared at me, and I knew she was furious.

Then she smiled, coldly. "Fine. May I know if you intend marrying her?"

I paused. "We have not talked about marriage yet, no."

She gave a curt nod. "And may I know the name of my grandchild's mother?"

I didn't want to tell her, but I couldn't think of a reason not to.

I told her.

"Thank you," she said. She didn't speak another word to me all dinner long and started talking to the gentleman on her other side. As soon as she had finished dessert, she got up to leave, without saying goodbye to me. She took long and expansive farewells from everyone else at the table. I watched my mother in her glamorous gown make her way through the room and thought I should leave with her, ensure she got the car and made it home all right. But I couldn't do it. The look on her face earlier that evening, filled me with dread. I didn't want to be alone in a car with her.

I left soon afterwards as well. I didn't want to call Lauren this late and the thought of going to my mother's house was simply too much, so I decided to get a room for the night. I walked up to reception and asked if they had free rooms. They only had an expensive suite available, and I took it.

It was only for a few hours, but it meant a night of peace and quiet.

I would have paid any price for that.

Chapter 17

Lauren

Halfway through the afternoon, my phone rang.

Caller ID was withheld.

"Is this Lauren Lambert?"

The voice on the other end of the line was cultivated and unmistakably female.

"Yes?"

"This is Cynthia Waterstone. I was hoping you would join me for tea on Friday afternoon."

Matthew's mother. I felt myself grow cold. He'd told me about the gala dinner and how she had reacted to the news.

"I have to work." It was the first thing that popped into my mind.

"What about Saturday morning then? Please, Lauren, I would really like to meet you."

She sounded nice, like an older lady who just wanted to talk to me.

It was my baby's grandmother. How could I say no?

But I was nervous all afternoon and the next morning I got up early, dressing conservatively in a high-necked blouse and a long skirt that was considerably tighter around my waistline.

"You look lovely," said my mother, approvingly. "I would love to have a daughter-in-law looking like that."

I gave her a look. "She doesn't want me for a daughter-in-law."

"How do you know that?" my mother smiled at me. Ever the optimist. Since she'd called Vic, on my advice, and found out he'd been in hospital with a kidney stone and therefore had been out of action for a few days, she was in a much better mood. The two of them were closer than ever and I could not remember when I had seen my mother so happy.

But I couldn't relax.

I was a few minutes early for our meeting and when the waiter took me to the table, I saw with a sinking heart that she was already there. Cynthia Waterstone rose as soon as she saw me, extending a long, cold hand that I had to shake.

"How do you do," she murmured, and I gave a quick smile.

She was probably the same age as my mother, perhaps in her late forties. But the similarity ended there. Cynthia Waterstone was poised and groomed. Her hair fell in styled waves from her face, which was carefully made up. She had no wrinkles, and her face was blemish-free. But the way her face looked was unnatural, somehow. Plastic surgery, I thought.

"Thank you for meeting me," she said and gave a tight smile. "I'm sure your weekends are very full, shopping for the baby."

The waiter came and she told him to bring us scones and tea. She didn't even ask what I wanted.

"Matthew was so secretive about the two of you!" She clasped her hands together and smiled, blinking a few times.

"I'm sure you understand, being his mother, I only want the best for him."

"Of course."

"You can imagine my shock when I heard he'd gotten himself mixed up in all of this!" She gave a delighted clap of the hands.

"What do you mean, mixed up?"

She leaned forward, as if we were two girlfriends sharing a secret. "Well, dear, you have no way of knowing if it's Matthew's child or not, do you?"

I stared at her, dumbstruck. "My sources tell me you were out with your boyfriend, Timothy Daxton, several times over that period. You were seen being very close and intimate. If I shared that information with Matthew, what do you think he would make of it?"

"You hired a PI to find dirt on me?" I asked incredulous.

"Of course not!" she waved my question away to show how silly I was being.

"All of this is so confusing! You falling pregnant unexpectedly, of course you don't know who the father is!"

"What..."

But she interrupted me. "Of course, Matthew is thrilled, but then he would be, being an only child! He'd always wanted siblings and now you've gone and made his dream come true! And as a prospective father, he does measure up much better than an aspiring musician with a drug problem, doesn't he?" she giggled as if she'd told a clever little joke.

I didn't know what to say.

"You know, of course, that Matthew comes from money. What is the colloquial term for it among your generation?" She pretended to think, then said, "Oh yes! Loaded! Not only from the Waterstone side of the family, but from my side as well. I was the sole heir to the Coolidge-Weston estate, so there is that too."

She smiled at me. "So, I was trying to think how much money I could offer you to go away and never contact Matthew again. I was thinking a hundred thousand dollars? But that sounds paltry, doesn't it? And you would have to leave your mother, start all over in a new place. So, would two hundred and fifty thousand dollars do it? A quarter of a million?"

She smiled at me, and it looked like a friendly smile. It really did. But when I looked carefully at her face, I could see how the smile ended on her mouth. Her eyes, the same dark shade as Matthew's, were not warm and inviting, as his were. Hers were cold and lifeless, like a muddy sort of quicksand, that wanted to swallow you and suck the life from you.

I got up slowly.

"We have a deal, yes?"

I turned around and walked out of the hotel, still unable to speak.

I knew that Cynthia Waterstone was a troubled woman, a person who had suffered great tragedy and unhappiness in her life. But I couldn't fathom the way she had spoken to me just now. The friendly, convivial way she had said the most insulting, horrible things and tried to bribe me; to get me to leave the city where I lived, where my mother was, just to get me out of her life. Of course, a quarter of a million dollars was a lot, I hardly knew how to wrap my head around a number like that. I could probably live off that for the rest of my life. But what kind of life would that be? Would it even be worth living?

When I later told my mother what had happened, she was gobsmacked too.

"She must really hate the thought of you having Matthew's baby," she said.

"You think?" We laughed and laughed, tears running down my face and I was so glad she was there to make me see the absurdity of the situation. There had been something malicious about Matthew's mother that I couldn't quite shake, but my mother's humorous take on the situation managed to take the sting out of it.

"I've been thinking," my mother said. "Maybe it's time I told you more about your real father."

I sat up, all ears. For years, I'd been begging her for this information, and she always came up with an excuse not to tell me.

As if reading my mind, she said, "I had a conversation with Vic about it and he pointed out that maybe it was time. He'd be the grandfather after all," she pulled up her shoulders.

Then she told me about how she met John Vickers, a music producer from Colorado, twenty-four years ago. He'd come up to New York to work on an album with a young musician collaborating with some local hip hop stars. On a night out with friends, he met my mother and they hit it off. He was in the city for only a few days, long enough to do a few takes and then he had to get back to his family in Denver. He'd told my mother all of this, how life as a young father was not what he signed up for, how the kids were cramping his style and his wife, now a nagging mom of two, was a far cry from the young singer he'd fallen for. My mother, a stunning young model, had secured a few good jobs and was quite taken with the older music producer, who she said, was awfully sexy and entertaining. She didn't want to wreck his family, she said, she just wanted to have fun.

"By the time I found out I was pregnant, he was long gone."

"And it could only have been him?"

She nodded. "I know I like to make out how wild and carefree I was back then, but really, after that week with him, I kind of took a break from the partying for a bit. I wanted to clear my head. So that is how I knew it had to be him. There wasn't anyone after John for quite some time."

I understood why she hadn't contacted him to tell him about me. Still, I was curious about him.

We looked him up on Facebook and I wasn't at all surprised to see that John Vickers had aged well. He still looked like a rocker, although he'd picked up a few pounds. I got his email address from his website and sent him an email, saying I was his daughter and that I'd like to get in touch, no strings attached, if he felt like it.

When I looked up, my mother stood in the kitchen, draining a glass of wine.

I went over to give her a hug.

"You okay?"

She nodded, but her cheeks were wet.

"All these years, I never told you his name. I don't know why, it became, this big thing. I don't know why," tears flowed down her cheeks.

"I know why," I said. "You raised me. Only you. And here I am," I said, beginning to cry too.

"You'll see, being a mother is the hardest job in the world," she said, smiling through her tears.

I suddenly thought of Cynthia Waterstone and shivered, as if someone had walked over my grave.

"You're thinking of Cruella, aren't you?" my mom said, and I started laughing again.

But later, I wondered how I could tell Matthew about his mom trying to pay me off, to get me out of town. He'd be furious and it would really affect his relationship with his mother even more. I was beginning to understand him so much better and after meeting his mother, I could see why he was emotionally so damaged. We had become much closer, and I was learning more about his childhood and about how he grew up.

He was always talking about giving the baby things he didn't have, but he wasn't talking about toys or swimming pools. He meant an attentive father, loving parents. We didn't have to be a family living in a picket-fence house with a golden-haired Labrador barking in the back yard.

He was so different with me too.

More open, sharing so much more. We hadn't slept together, not again, but I'd been thinking about it. I wanted to and I knew he did too. But I wanted to be careful, not rush into things. With the baby on the way, I wanted to grow up a little, I guess.

I knew my life was about to change and I was still nervous about it.

Especially after meeting Cynthia Waterstone. The thought that I was giving her a grandchild, gave me goosebumps. Literally. I couldn't shake the feeling that the woman was evil and that I needed to get as far away from her as possible. Was it possible that she could snatch the baby after it was born? I didn't know if my mind was playing tricks on me or if I really had to consider the possibility of her planning something.

Then there was Matthew. I didn't know how he would react to her little web of lies designed to trick him, playing on the jealous streak she must have known he had. How far would she go to convince Matthew I was only trying to trap him?

Chapter 18

Matthew

The following week I had to travel to Hamburg.

I wasn't keen on the trip to Germany, but the health market here was strong and there were indications we could expand on our distribution. I had already managed to get us into the UK and the numbers were looking good. I was meeting some officials from the European Union as well. I didn't speak to Lauren over the weekend, but we exchanged brief messages.

I called her on Tuesday night, but she didn't answer. I left a message. She didn't get back to me.

Same thing on Wednesday night.

Something felt off.

I called her at work, something I had never done before.

The switchboard put me through to Diaz.

"Mr. Waterstone! How're the Germans!"

"Very German," I responded, rather curtly. "Where's Lauren?"

"She took a few days leave, personal business?"

"Thank you."

I sent her a text, asking her to call me urgently.

She answered briefly.

Call u 2nite.

I had an excellent dinner with some representatives from the European Union and discussions on shipping our products to member states. Yet, I couldn't enjoy my successful meetings. I was worried about Lauren and why she wasn't at work. I went back to my office and decided to call her instead of waiting for her to call me.

"Matthew?"

"Lauren! I haven't heard from you, what's going on?"

"I'm fine."

"Diaz said you took leave?"

"I was going to tell you," she said, sounding a bit evasive.

"Tell me what?"

"My mother told me the name of my father. I emailed him last week, saying I'd like to meet him, and he responded, inviting me to come and visit him."

"When was this?"

"Last weekend, as you were leaving for Europe. By the way, how's Germany?"

"Fine, everything is fine here," I said, distracted. "But, okay... tell me about this visit."

"I decided to put in some leave, and I flew to Denver on Monday!" she sounded excited.

"Wait a minute... you're there already?" I couldn't believe I didn't know this. "Why didn't you tell me?"

"It happened so fast, and I wanted to talk to you over the phone, but we weren't able to talk yet," she said, again sounding reserved, unlike her usual self.

"Is everything okay?" I asked.

"Yes! Of course!"

"How's the baby?"

"Still growing," Lauren said, and I felt somewhat reassured.

"So, what's he like, your father?" I asked.

"Let me just go outside..." she said, trying to get some privacy. After a moment, she went on.

"He's... not exactly what I thought! I mean, he's friendly and very laidback! He's got this farmhouse on some land outside the city. I have my own guest suite. It's awesome. I've got a half-sister named Ava, who's two years older than me. We clicked right away, I'm so happy I came!"

"Wait a minute... Lauren? When are you coming back?" I don't know what made me ask this. "You left so suddenly, without saying anything and now it sounds like, I don't know? Are you sure everything is fine?"

There was a long silence on the other end of the line.

"I don't know how to tell you this," she finally said.

"What is it?"

Then she told me about my mother asking to meet her and how she tried to pay off Lauren to leave town. With my baby. She told me about my mother hiring a PI to dig into Lauren's past and try to find out incriminating information about her.

"Oh, my God, Lauren, I can't believe she did that."

But I could. That was the sad truth. My mother would do anything, not for me, but for the son she wanted. It was like she had been fighting her whole life to squeeze me into a certain mold, hoping I'd take the shape she wanted. With some things, it had worked. Mostly, I let her have her way. But not this.

"She hates me, Matthew. She will never allow me to be in your life," Lauren said quietly.

"It's not up to her," I said. "You have to believe me."

"I do," Lauren said, sounding miserable. "But you live in the same house, your lives are so connected."

"I will talk to her. If she doesn't come round, I will move out."

"I don't want to come between you and your mother."

I couldn't believe we were having this conversation.

"So, this is why you left?"

"I wanted to get away, think about everything. I felt like I couldn't breathe in the office, knowing she could come to the door at any moment."

"I'm flying back tomorrow," I said. "I'm going to sort this out."

I was meant to stay a few days longer, but I had already had the most important meetings. All I could think about now, was getting back and sorting out this mess with my mother.

On the flight back, I kept thinking about the year after my father died. How my mother had sent me away to live with my grandparents. They were kind, decent people, but much older and I was a desperately unhappy boy and alone. My grandfather took me fishing and I remember him patting my back awkwardly, saying I was going to be fine. Neither him nor my grandmother knew how to comfort or talk to me. I heard them at night, talking about me, worrying about me. The following year, I stayed with my father's brother, Albert, and his wife Kathy. Their three sons, all rambunctious and loud, sporty types accepted me into the fold. I found a way to live with them, but as I grew older, I preferred going back to boarding school and being by myself. My mother employed an older woman called Frances to run the household. Frances was short and very upright, with stiff wiry hair. She became a kind of substitute mother for me, making me hot chocolate and asking after school when I came home for the holidays. She made me sit down and tell her about the boys in my class, my subjects, and which ones I liked and which ones I didn't. She stroked my hair while I sat at the kitchen table. I brought her chocolate that I bought from the vending machine at school. Then, when I was seventeen, I came home one year to find someone else in the kitchen.

"Where's Frances?" I asked. The woman told me to ask my mother.

My mother sat at her dressing table, fixing her hair for an evening out. "Frances died. Turns out she had cancer, never said a word. Fell over one day, just like that." My mother's voice, so cold and disconnected, shocked me.

"You didn't tell me!"

My mother's eyebrows lifted in an expression of surprise. "Why would I?"

"I would have liked to go to her funeral!" I remember struggling to hide my sadness from my mother.

"Don't be absurd!"

I thought her heartless and a snob.

I knew where Frances's family lived. She'd told me once. I found the ramshackle house in the Bronx where her brother Joe and his family lived. I knocked on their door and Joe's wife Macy opened the door. When I told her who I was, she invited me in, made me sit down at her kitchen table, offered me tea. She told me about Frances's illness, about the cancer that had spread quickly and how she had told nobody about it until it was too late for treatment.

"She loved you," Macy said to me, covering my hand with hers. "She always told me how you brought her something whenever you came back from school. She loved those candies more than you'll ever know."

Even then, I didn't allow myself to cry. I couldn't show this kind woman how much Frances had meant to me.

"In the end, she talked about you a lot. She wanted to say goodbye to you, but she didn't know how to contact you at school, she didn't want to upset you. She knew Mrs. Waterstone wouldn't like it." Macy got up and fetched something from another room. She came back with a mug that I had once gifted Frances over Christmas, it was a cheap gift shop purchase that simply said I love you, with a red heart in place of the word love.

"After she collapsed, she came back here. She had only a few things. This was among her belongings."

I had never confronted my mother about her coldness, and her inhuman treatment of Frances, who had been such a comfort to me when she could not. But finding out what she had tried to do with Lauren, brought it all back again.

When I arrived home, she wasn't there.

The housekeeper, Rosario, said she'd gone out.

I waited for her in her sitting room upstairs, and as soon as I heard her coming up the stairs, I went out to meet her.

"Matthew, you're back."

"I want to talk to you."

"I'll ring for some tea," she said.

I ignored her. "You tried to bribe Lauren."

A steely resolve set among her features. "I only tried to do what is best for you."

"No, you tried to do what is best for you."

"You're tired from your flight, you're not seeing clearly."

"On the contrary, I am seeing things very clearly." I paused. "Don't make me choose between her and you."

"That shouldn't even be a choice!" my mother declared. "Lauren Lambert is a common slut! That isn't your child! I spoke to the real father, an absolute dead beat!"

"Don't talk about Lauren like that! I won't have it!"

She glared at me. "You are a Waterstone. You will marry well. Carry this family's name forward."

"If you cannot accept Lauren, I am walking out this door and you will not see me again."

"You wouldn't dare!"

"You underestimate me, Mother!" I saw my mother's face react to the news, but I didn't care.

"Lauren is my future and I intend being with her. If you can't accept it there will be no place for you in it!"

I went down the stairs and she shouted after me. "What about your father, Matthew? He died for this company, for you! Would you really do this to me, to his memory? After everything we have gone through? You will bring shame to this family!"

I heard her voice as I went into my room, slamming the door behind me. Despite my resolve, I was shaken by her words. I took a few things from my room, packed the most important items, then decided to come back for the rest. I had to get out of there. I looked at what had been my bedroom for most of my life. It had been renovated when I took over at Egal and it looked so impersonal, like a suite at a hotel. No wonder I was so comfortable in hotel rooms. I thought of Lauren's apartment, the photographs of happy times stuck against the fridge, the framed children's art, the hand painted clay pots and fraying rugs on the floor.

When I came out the door, my mother stood at the front door, her cheeks wet, and I had to resist the urge to touch them to see if they were real.

"Don't do this, Matthew, I beg you," she said. "If not for me, then do it for your father. Please don't leave."

"Father wanted me to be happy," I said. "I've never been happy here."

I pushed past her and opened the front door, and a cold gust of air greeted me in the face.

Chapter 19

The first morning I woke up in Colorado, I was completely disoriented. It was the light and the silence. I got up and went into the main house, thrown by all the space and the absence of the hustle and bustle of New York. I'd grown up with the city, was used to the sound of traffic and honking car horns, sirens and people yelling to one another across the street.

Here, it was just, so quiet.

It was weird.

"You're up!" I turned around and saw John, my father, walking towards me with a big grin.

"You going to have some coffee?" He had a big booming voice to go with his towering six-foot frame.

"Thanks."

I was still getting used to the idea of him as my father. To begin with, he had a huge beard and a deep, gravelly voice. He made me think of an ageing cowboy, but in a good way. A rough diamond, and at least fifteen years older than my mother. He'd insisted on fetching me from the airport, saying the drive out to the farm could be confusing for strangers. I had feared conversation would be uncomfortable, but he launched right in.

"I have to tell you; I wasn't that surprised to hear from you."

"Really?"

He grinned at me, a little shamefaced. "I'd heard from some of our mutual acquaintances that Ellie had gotten pregnant soon after my visit to the Big Apple. I wondered if I might be the father." He paused. "I tried calling her, but she wouldn't answer."

My mother had not told me that.

"Look, she knew I was married, and our thing, was kind of a fling, I guess…"

"She never wanted to tell me who you were. I only found out your name a few days ago," I said. "I couldn't figure out why she'd kept it a secret."

John nodded. "She was drop dead gorgeous back then," he said.

I nodded. I'd seen pictures of my mother from her modeling days.

"She's still a looker," I said with a smile.

"I bet!" I wondered if John still carried a torch for my mother. He wouldn't be the first.

"We're very close," I said. "She's been the best mother."

"You're a great kid, so she must have done something right," he said.

Then he said, "You've got two half siblings, Vern and Ava, you'll meet them tonight."

"Your wife?"

He cleared his throat. "We got divorced ten years ago. Guess she had enough of my wandering ways."

"You cheated on her?"

"Guilty as charged, ma'am," he tried to laugh it off, then he became serious. "Ah, I don't know what to tell you. I did some things I'm not proud of, I'll own up to that."

I didn't know what to make of him. The farm, on the outskirts of Denver, had belonged to his parents. He'd sold off some of the land and renovated the house with money from the studio, which he said had done well over the years. I had a feeling just how well, when I saw the large house and the horses in the paddock across the field.

"It's beautiful," I said when I got out of the car and took in the view. John smiled, proud.

Ava and Vern were waiting for us. Both were tall, like their father and Vern had short hair and a clean-cut face. Ava was shorter, with lively blue eyes, very much like my own. Both greeted me warmly, but I sensed some wariness. John showed me to the guest room, an enormous room with a bathroom and my own little porch overlooking the mountains.

"What a view! Wow!"

I was blown away by all of it.

Ava and Vern stayed for dinner, which they helped to cook with their father. It was steak and potatoes, a salad, and some pumpkin from the garden. The three of them talked the whole time, telling me about life on the farm, growing up with their parents, then after the divorce, how they moved back and forth between their parents. Both kids were in high school already and didn't seem too traumatized by it.

But later, when I helped with the washing up, Ava said to me, "He was a good father, but a terrible husband. They were always fighting, and I remember my mother crying a lot when I was growing up. I was relieved when they decided to call it quits."

"How is she now?"

"She got remarried to a Christian fundamentalist," Vern said, coming into the kitchen and rolling his eyes. "It gets a bit heavy going around the house sometimes."

"Oh, go on!" Ava shoved her brother good-naturedly, "Mom is happy!"

Vern nodded.

"And you two, what do you do?"

Vern was the sales director at a furniture business in town and Ava worked at a PR company. Her job sounded interesting, and we had a lot to talk about. After Vern went home and John went to bed, the two of us sat down to unwind. I told her about my life, the drama around the pregnancy and Matthew.

"No wonder you were so quick to get out of there!" she laughed.

"It felt like a good time to take a break," I admitted. "I'd always wondered about my father, what he was like."

"And how do you find him?" she asked.

I was honest. "I guess it's hard not to like him, in spite of everything."

"That's true," she said. "Mom used to say it was the music business and mixing with the big names, all the partying. All the drugs and the drinking, there were so many women and I guess dad really likes the ladies." She rolled her eyes and I laughed.

"Is there anyone in his life now?"

"Not that I know of," she said. "He's had a health scare with high blood pressure. I think he is trying to be healthier. But I'd be very surprised if he tried to mend his ways now. Dad's a bit of a bad boy, always was."

"Don't tell him about the pregnancy yet," I said. "I'll get round to it, eventually."

"You're keeping it?"

"Yes."

"But why?"

I knew what she meant. With Matthew's mother making it difficult and us not exactly being a model couple, not to mention how young I was and only starting out in my career; it didn't seem like a good time.

"It's hard to explain," I said. "But it's this idea of a new life, growing inside of me. It has to be a good thing, you know?"

"Can't you just get a puppy?"

I had to laugh, I really liked Ava, she was direct and funny in a way that was not unlike me. We had taken to each other and when she invited me to lunch the next day, I was keen to go. John gave me a lift to town and said he'd pick me up afterwards. I asked him about the blood pressure scare but he waved my question away.

"Oh, you know the doctors... They have to make money somehow."

"You're not taking it seriously?"

"You've got to live before you die, and I can tell you I am not done living yet!"

"Don't you want to be around to meet your grandchild?" I patted my stomach, which was beginning to show.

"You're pregnant?! Holy cow!" he seemed delighted by the news. Both his children had not shown any signs of settling down yet, he said, and he hit the steering wheel a few times, making me laugh at his exuberance. It was hard not to like him. John Vickers may not have been great husband or father material, but he was a force of positivity and good humor. You couldn't help wanting to be around him and enjoying his company.

Later in the car, when we came back from my lunch, he said, "Look, this is all new, our father-daughter thing. I don't know what the set-up is with the daddy, but I would like to help."

"That's, uhm, real nice of you," I said. "Things are complicated but I'm all right."

"I didn't have the opportunity to be a father to you, but I'd like to be a grandfather, if you'll let me?"

"Definitely," I said.

I thought of how I'd enjoyed Ava showing me around her office, introducing me to her colleagues as her sister, the way everyone here had welcomed me. There was none of the suspicion and distrust that I'd seen from Matthew's mother. I wondered if we would ever be able to get past the moment where she had offered me money to disappear from her son's life, taking her grandchild from me.

I tried to find sympathy for her, but it was hard.

Matthew had painted a picture of a woman who lived for the memory of her dead husband, unable to see her son for the person that he was. I understood him so much better now. Inside, he was still a wounded boy, hiding his true self because he didn't know how to heal himself, how to pick himself up and move on. All he knew, was how to circle the wagons and close the doors, keeping people out.

It sometimes felt like he wanted the baby almost as much as I did, and I knew he would help me take care of it. But I didn't know if he could stand up to his mother and what she would do if he tried to resist her. She had a kind of hold over him and I knew that it had been only the two of them for so long, and even in this unhealthy set-up, this was what Matthew knew.

The Cynthia Waterstone I'd met was used to getting what she wanted.

And I was in her way.

Chapter 20

Matthew

The next board meeting was nasty.

For all of us.

Egal was a family business and most of the board members consisted of family: my mother, my uncle Albert and his cousin, Bill Bouvier. Then there was a woman, Geraldine Fraser, who represented my mother's side of the business, in particular her father and his investment. The last board member, apart from myself, was a well-known venture capitalist in the city, Gregory Dawn. Of all the board members, he could usually be relied on for the most informed business opinions.

I waited for them in our usual meeting room, as I didn't want to walk into my mother outside. We had not seen each other since the fight at the house a week ago. I'd moved into a hotel room and had my PA fetch the rest of my clothes in the week. My mother had not called me, and I had not contacted her either.

When the board members arrived, I detected unease in their postures, the way especially the family members avoided my eyes and quickly shook my hand. I was on good terms with all of them, at least, I always had been.

I was filled with a sense of foreboding and started off with the usual feedback on issues the board were interested in. Then I reported back about my trip to Europe, and they were pleased to hear about the progress made with the expansion plans for the EU member states. I addressed all of the board members, as I spoke, taking care not to engage my mother directly but not ignore her either.

At the end of the meeting, my uncle suddenly spoke.

"There is one more item on the agenda."

He looked down at his hands, he seemed very uncomfortable. I noticed the other board members shifting in their seats. Except for my mother, she was sitting up very straight, staring straight at me.

"It's come to our attention, Matthew, that a junior member of the company has fallen pregnant and is apparently claiming you are responsible."

"How is this any concern of the board?"

Geraldine Fraser, my mother's puppet, spoke up, "This is a family business as you are aware, the company vision and mission statement prioritize family values. Our reputation has always been extremely important. Health being not only physically, but mentally, socially, and ethically balanced as well."

"I still don't see the relevance," I said stiffly, keeping my temper under control. This was my mother's doing, I was sure of it. I had to remain calm at all costs.

"Matthew." My uncle, who was sitting next to me, leaned over, dropping his voice in an attempt to convey sympathy, I think.

"There is some concern that this girl could bring bad publicity to the company. She could claim sexual harassment, spark media interest in our company culture. We don't want this kind of exposure as I'm sure you'll understand."

"What do you mean?" I asked, addressing him directly.

"She needs to leave the company, with a handsome package of course. You need to distance yourself from her, you must have no contact. We don't want another Oliveira incident."

He was referring to the sales director, Peter de Oliveira who two years ago, shot and killed his wife in an apparent crime of passion. Even though it had happened at home, the result of an ugly divorce and had nothing to do with work, the media spent several weeks exploring his personal life and that of his wife, highlighting their extravagant lifestyles and casting the company in a rather negative light. There were suggestions that either Egal paid him too much or made him work too hard, neglecting his wife and family. There was no truth to those rumors, of course. His wife was having an affair and wanted to leave him, a fact that Peter would not accept. The murder was a tragedy, but it had nothing to do with work.

"No, we don't want press coverage," I said.

"We're agreed then? You will take care of this?"

I nodded.

The meeting was adjourned, and the board members left quickly, eager to get out of there. I stayed behind, turning my back to the door so that I wouldn't have to watch them leave.

"Matthew?"

I turned around. My uncle Albert was standing at the table, his hands in his pockets.

"I'm sorry about that," he said.

"I'm guessing, my mother had a hand in this?"

He nodded. "She's been calling us all week, putting pressure on the board to speak up."

"She tried to buy Lauren off too, thinking if she threw enough money at her she'd take the baby and disappear from my life."

"Your mother..."

"Please," I interrupted him coldly, "I don't want lectures from you about my mother."

Uncle Albert was a big man, a kind man. He'd lost much of his hair, picked up a lot of weight, but his eyes were still warm, albeit a bit sad. He'd always tried to be there for me over the years, but he was mindful of not overstepping his place. He'd often told me he didn't want to pretend to be my father and I appreciated his tact.

"I didn't deserve that," I told him. "Besides, Lauren is great at her job. Yes, she happens to be pregnant, and I am the father. But there is no risk to the company."

"Even so," Uncle Albert said gently, "It could get out. The news, I mean. A financial journalist may get it into their head to attack us this way."

"I've had enough of this," I said, firmly. "Are you saying the board is losing confidence in me?"

"No, no, not at all," my uncle spoke quickly, anxiously. "You are doing a marvelous job, Matthew, we are all very happy. It's just... your mother, you know, she's worried, and I wanted to bring it up."

"You mean, she wanted you to bring it up."

I was furious with my mother for manipulating Uncle Albert and with him as well, for allowing himself to be used.

"Look, I am happy for you," my uncle finally said. "If this is what you want."

"It is."

"Then this is wonderful news. But think about how it could look for the company."

This was the last straw. The fact that he thought I needed reminding of the bloody business that had overshadowed my whole life. I had never been allowed to think of anything or anyone else.

"I don't give a damn about that!"

I saw his eyes widen in shock. I'd never spoken to him like that.

I turned around and left without saying another word to him. My pulse was racing, and I felt an uncontrollable rage. There was no way I could go back to the office like this. I needed to get out, clear my head.

I went down to the parking garage, got my car, and called my PA, cancelling my meetings for the rest of the day. "I am going to put in a few days of sick leave, that shouldn't be a problem. Can you take care of that?"

"Sure, yes."

"Is there anything urgent on my diary, anything that can't wait?"

She looked at my calendar and there was nothing that urgent.

"What's going on?" she asked.

I hesitated. "I need some time off. It's personal, but if anyone asks, say it's a medical break. Hemorrhoid surgery. That should shut them up."

"Does this have anything to do with Lauren?"

"What do you know about Lauren?" I asked sharply.

"People talk around here, I've heard that the two of you were seen one weekend, holding hands?"

"Thanks for keeping me updated on the office gossip," I said dryly, ending the call.

I put a call through to the company vice-president, my other cousin Will. We weren't exactly close, but we'd learnt to get along over the years. I told him I was taking a few days off and leaving him in charge.

"This have anything to do with the girl downstairs?"

Of course, he'd know.

"Did your father talk to you?"

"It's your mother," he said with a chuckle. "She's been talking to everyone she can, trying to get us on her side.

"I've had it with her," I said, my voice shaking with anger. "This is my personal life; it's got nothing to do with her or the company!"

"It is a family business, as I don't need to remind you!" he said, rather lightly.

"Jesus, Will. I have heard nothing but the family business all my life. Every conversation, my entire life. I'm sick of it!"

I knew I shouldn't be talking like this to the company VP, but Will was also a friend. We'd play softball together when we were younger, gone to a few games together. He was engaged to a girl from the city. No great beauty, as my mother put it, but she had seemed nice to me when we met.

"I get it," Will said. "You need a break. You haven't had a few days since I don't know when. What'll you do?"

"Maybe go up to the cabin. Get away from the air conditioning, the carpeted corridors."

"Sounds like a good idea. And you know, Matthew?"

"Yeah?"

"We've got your back. The board won't force you to do anything."

"How do you know?"

"My dad told me. He said he raised the issue as a courtesy to your mother, but if she really wants to take it further, there will be no support from the board. Geraldine may try something, but they will be outvoted."

"Good."

"Take a few days, I'll hold the fort."

I ended the call and thought about what he'd said. I wondered if Will was looking forward to stepping up as acting CEO, if he had designs on my job. It wouldn't have surprised me. All the talk of it being a family business and family values didn't fool me for a minute. There was a lot of money at stake and if Albert could get his son in the driving seat, I was sure he would support such a move.

I drove to my hotel to pack a few things.

My phone pinged. It was Lauren, sending me a picture of herself on her father's farm.

Missing you x

I saw Lauren smiling at me, a natural glow on her cheeks, a big smile on her face. The little kiss at the end of her message was an afterthought. But it was this gesture, this little bit of sweetness that made me change my mind.

About everything.

Instead of heading north, I got a cab and asked to be taken to the airport.

Chapter 21

Lauren

After a few days in Colorado, I was beginning to feel that it was time to go.

John had been very welcoming, but he needed to get back to work and I didn't like spending all day alone at home on the farm. However, I wasn't ready to go back to the city yet.

I wanted to have a solution to my situation or at least an idea of how to approach the future. But nothing presented itself. I wanted to be with Matthew, and he wanted to be with me, but his mother was a dark presence overshadowing us.

I mentioned this to my mother over the phone.

"You're being paranoid!" my mother said to me over the phone. "Come back! I don't want you having that baby in Colorado!"

Ava wanted me to stay longer, she told me her company could find some work for me if I wanted to get out of the city for longer. They were working on a series of children's books, and she thought I could be client liaison. It was a tempting offer, but I didn't want to overdo it with my new family here either. I had taken a cab back to the farm and thought that I needed to come up with a plan soon. I was feeling much stronger now, the nausea had passed, and I had some of my former energy back. Perhaps I could go back to work, with a taser in my bag? As my taxi came up the drive, I saw a strange luxury car in front of the house. Perhaps one of John's clients? I paid my driver, got out and saw a man leaning against the car, clearly waiting. He turned around and my heart skipped a beat.

"Matthew?"

A big grin broke over his face. He gave a few strides, swept me into his arms and kissed me.

"Hello, you!"

"What are you doing here?!" I laughed.

He pulled up his shoulders and laughed too. "I decided it was time for a break. I thought I'd join you up here, sweep you away for a romantic break in the mountains, what do you say?"

It sounded fantastic, of course.

"But what about work?"

A shadow crossed his face. "I'll tell you all about it later," he said.

I told him I had to wait for John to get back from work to say a proper goodbye. I also texted Ava, who said she would come by after work.

"You can show me around," Matthew said, and I couldn't get over how relaxed he looked. He was dressed casually, in slim fit jeans and a silky sweater. He smiled a lot, kept touching me, pulling me close.

"I've missed you," he said, when he noticed me looking at him. "The city has been lonely without you."

I wasn't used to him being this expressive, I didn't know what to say.

Suddenly, he seemed anxious, "Maybe I shouldn't have come? Is it too much?"

"No, no! Not at all! I'm happy to see you," I reassured him.

I was happy to see him. It had been almost two weeks since I'd seen him and so much had happened in my life. But I liked the idea of going somewhere else, with him, before we went back to New York.

"You're looking well," he said. "How're you feeling?"

"I think I'm beginning to show!" I said, patting my little tummy. I was past the three months mark, into my second trimester. I had started wearing looser tops and had found a cowboy-style shirt in a Denver shop that was very comfortable. I packed my things and we waited for John and Ava in the living room. Saying goodbye to them was harder than I thought it would be.

Ava had tears in her eyes and made me promise to email her. John was uncomfortable, pulling me into a big bear hug.

"You bring that little grand baby round to see her granddaddy, all right?"

Then he turned to Matthew. "You look after her, you hear?"

Matthew solemnly promised to do that.

Then we got into the hired car and headed for the mountains.

"I thought we both deserved something special," Matthew said to me as we drove off the farm. "So, I thought a spa hotel, in the mountains, private, but super luxurious."

"Sounds fantastic!"

Then I said, "What's been going on in the city?"

Matthew didn't answer straight away.

"Please tell me, Matthew, I want to know what's going on."

He told me about the fight with his mother, and that he'd moved out. When he gave me the details about the board meeting and how that had gone down, I was horrified.

"So, everyone knows at work? They're all talking about us?"

He grimaced. "Looks like it."

"And there is talk of me suing the company? Holy cow. How will I be able to face them?" I wondered out loud.

"Do you want to?"

"What do you mean?"

"It's totally your choice, but you don't have to work, you know. I'll support you. Or, if you want to work, work wherever you want. You could take a break from the company if you wanted to."

I grew quiet. "Is this your way of saying I have to resign?"

"No! Not at all! If you want to keep working there, that's totally fine!"

I wanted to believe him. I was still mulling it over when he said, "Actually, I've been thinking I might quit."

"What?" This was a shocking development. Matthew loved his job, being the boss. It was all he had ever talked about, being the CEO of Egal, taking over from his father.

"I don't know. I've just been thinking... "

Our conversation was interrupted by a sign for the hotel, and we took the next turn off. The road snaked off into the mountains and it was hard not to be distracted by the stunning mountain scenery. The resort was quite deep in the mountains, surrounded by thick vegetation. There was a main lodge and several smaller cabins, hidden amongst the trees of a pine forest. Elevated wooden walkways connected the cabins to the main lodge and gave the impression of being up in the foliage, like tree houses.

"This is amazing!" I said, my breath taken away by the exquisite log cabins.

"Did you see the bathrooms?" Matthew asked me, a naughty grin on his face. "I saw this place online, I figured it looked amazing."

But I was walking through the living room and into the bedroom, which had a big glass wall looking out directly over the forest. There was a drop into the forest floor so it was completely private, there was no way anyone could walk past the window and see you. This view of leaves and branches, birds flitting from tree to tree was mesmerizing.

"There is only one bedroom, but I figured I'll take the couch," Matthew said, pointing to a wide sofa in the living room. I gave him a look.

"Really, I don't mind. I asked for a two-roomed unit, but they didn't have one and I didn't want to miss out."

I realized he was being serious. He really had tried to find a two-bedroomed cabin so I wouldn't assume we'd sleep together. He would bring me to a place like this, the epitome of romance and not expect me to put out.

Was this where I fell in love with him? Properly, deeply?

Maybe.

I certainly fell in lust with him. Perhaps my hormones were going wild, I had heard about that happening during pregnancy. Because all I could suddenly think about, was the two of us getting naked.

He sat on the couch, testing it out with his hand and calling out to me that it was fine and that he would be able to sleep there.

"Matthew?"

"Yes?"

"Would you come here please?"

He came to the bedroom, where I was lying on the bed. "Come feel this mattress, tell me what you think."

I saw him hesitate, wondering what I was playing at. But I kept my face straight, pretending to press down on the coverlet. "I'm not sure if this bed will do."

"Really?"

He came over, leaned down to touch it. I reached up and grabbed his arm, pulling him down on the bed. He fell next to me on the bed, laughing. He smelled clean, spicy and I was overcome with a rush of desire for him. With his day-old stubble, those dark, smoldering eyes, he was so attractive. I couldn't believe we were here, all alone, in this stunning cabin. I leaned over him and kissed him, hungry, and sensing his hesitation, pulled back.

"Not what you had in mind?" I asked.

"No... I mean... yes! But what about the baby?"

"What about the baby?" I asked, kissing him again, enjoying the delicious sensation of his mouth opening, his tongue finding mine and an almost aching sensation in my groin. I slipped my top off and took my pants off. "Have you heard about how some pregnant women become super horny?"

Matthew was laughing, shaking his head. I could see he was surprised by my sudden behavior, but it clearly was a pleasant one judging from the bulge in his pants.

"I can't tell," I pouted. "Are my breasts bigger yet?" I pulled my bra off and he was all over me in seconds, pushing me back against the bed, kissing me and caressing my breasts. I groaned with pleasure; I could hardly stand the anticipation of waiting for him. He took off his clothes, grinning madly, before holding me against him, tightly, skin to skin. He ran his hands down my body, lay down on the bed and pulled me on top of him. I didn't mind, I liked being on top. I felt voluptuous and gorgeous, my breasts so tender to the touch, and when he came up to kiss my breasts, gently biting my nipples, I thought I was going to come.

I moved on top of his body, rubbing my body against his cock, teasing both of us until I couldn't bear it anymore. I slipped him inside of me and rocked back and forth feeling the pressure build in powerful waves. I leaned back and felt my orgasm coming, wondrous waves of passion that rocked my body, making me moan and whimper, sounds I had never made before in my life. I felt him shudder with me and realized we'd come together. I fell back onto the bed, exhausted, a smile of total bliss on my face.

After a few moments, I said, "What are the dinner plans at this place?"

"Are you hungry?"

"Starving!" I said. "I'm eating for two now, remember?"

"Let's order room service," he said. "That way we don't have to get out of bed at all."

He grinned at me, wickedly, clearly ready for another round.

Chapter 22

Matthew

I woke up the following morning, not knowing where I was for a moment.

I opened my eyes and saw Lauren, waking up at about the same time.

She looked absolutely gorgeous; her blue eyes darker than usual, still heavy with sleep. Her lips curled into a slow smile.

"How'd you sleep?"

"I don't know..." I said. "I think that sofa would've been more comfortable."

"Liar!" she shoved me playfully and I caught her in my arms, kissing her quickly. Her lips softened and she caught my bottom lip between her teeth in a gentle bite.

"Ouch!" I laughed and kissed her back.

Our kiss became more intense, I pushed back the covers to take her in my arms again, holding her tightly. We made love more slowly this time, savoring each other. I took my time with her, caressing her body, loving the smoothness of her skin, the new curves of her body, the gentle rise of her small bump, before sliding my hand between her legs, slipping inside of her. She groaned with pleasure, and I felt her grow wetter. I parted her legs and she twisted them around me, urging me closer. The bliss as I entered her overwhelmed me, the pleasure building as I thrust deeper into her.

Afterwards, holding her in my arms, she leaned back to kiss me.

"I think we should stay in bed all day," she said.

"I second that motion," I said.

"When do you have to get back to work?"

I stiffened without meaning to. The thought of the office and what was waiting for me back in the city was too unpleasant.

"I'm sorry," she said quickly, turning around to land butterfly kisses on my mouth.

"Have I spoiled the mood?" I didn't say anything but sat up in the bed. She looked pensive. I pulled her closer. Through the large glass window, we looked at the surrounding forest, and the lush greenery calmed me. I was far away from work, from my office. I knew I couldn't hold it against Lauren for being pragmatic. She didn't know that this was my first proper holiday in a very long time, probably in years.

"We'll have to go back eventually, I guess," I reluctantly said.

"But I've been thinking..." I hadn't really had time to think about it too much, but over the past few days a thought had taken root in my mind that I was struggling to get rid of.

I decided to say it out loud.

"What if I quit my job? Resigned as CEO of Egal?"

"To do what?"

I shrugged. "Anything."

I didn't really have financial worries. I had not told Lauren the extent of my personal wealth, but it was substantial. I had inherited a large amount from my father, most of which had been invested. As I'd been living with my mother in the family home, I'd not had to buy a property and had not wasted my inheritance on flashy parties or overseas trips. I'd been investing in the stock market, playing with trades and betting on some rather wild ventures. Some didn't pan out. But others did. If I was careful, I didn't have to work, ever again. Neither did she.

"I took the job as CEO of Egal for my mother's sake. But she went too far, with you. And then trying to turn the board against me. That was a low blow."

"What about the family name, the Waterstone legacy?"

I put my hand on her belly.

"This is the Waterstone legacy."

I saw her blinking at me.

"I don't think my father intended for the company to become the kind of toxic environment it has become, a place where the family fights, like dogs with a bone.

I took a breath. "From what I remember about my father, he was more playful, not that serious. Take the accident that killed him? It was his passion that plane. But he had not that long before received his pilot's license. He could be reckless sometimes."

"What happened, with the plane?"

"I don't know, we think he accidentally flew into power cables. The plane crashed into the ground. There was a fire, his body was burnt beyond recognition."

"That's terrible!"

"I once overheard my cousins joking that maybe it wasn't him at all. That maybe he'd staged his death to get away from my mother, the family, and the fighting about the company."

"Your mother?!"

"I know…" I didn't really know what they meant, and I couldn't ask them. But over the years, I had often wondered if my mother's description of their marriage and relationship was not a little idealized. One of the board members, Bill Bouvier, had over the years made references to my father's drinking. He'd said on occasion that my father was fond of making rash business decisions late at night, halfway through a bottle of bourbon. He also said my father was always picking hobbies that took him away from work. I didn't like the sound of that.

"What did they mean about the fighting about the company?"

"I asked my Uncle Albert once; he didn't like talking about it. But it seemed that he'd been the CEO of the company originally. But when my mother's father invested in the company, one of his conditions had been that my father take over the day-to-day running of the business."

"Your uncle must've hated that."

I knew he did. Even though Albert had always been friendly towards me, he was reluctant to talk about my father. When I became

CEO, I suggested he become chairman of the board, a powerful position that he seemed to enjoy. Perhaps he was ready to take over again. Or maybe he would encourage Will to fill the position. I found that I didn't really care, one way or another.

"I feel as if the company has controlled my life for long enough," I said. "I'm ready to start something new."

"You won't miss it?" Lauren asked.

"I don't think so. The last few days have been very liberating," I gave a laugh and kissed her again, feeling my good mood from earlier returning. "Being away from it, and with you, is the happiest I have been in ages. I don't want to give it up."

"If it is up to me, you don't have to," she said with a tender smile.

We spent the day in bed, ordering room service and talking about the past.

We connected in a way we had never been able to do before. Away from our families, from the company and all the responsibilities that always seemed to overshadow us, we could be together without any impediments. We had sex, talked, drank non-alcoholic champagne, and thought up names for our baby.

"I suppose you'll have to give a family name?" Lauren said. "I'm not sure I like Cynthia though."

I shook my head. "God, no."

I thought about my grandmother and the cookies she had baked for me after my father's death. Batch after batch of rather hard, inedible cookies that were her way of trying to cheer me up. I could see now that they probably didn't know how to deal with me. They had lost a son too and were in mourning too without having to deal with a moody grandson.

"What about Elizabeth?" I said, "My grandmother's name?"

"We could call her Beth," Lauren said with a smile. "But what if it's a boy? What was your grandfather's name?"

"Jonathan."

"I like that."

I felt a rush of emotion that caught me by surprise. Was this what love felt like? I had never felt like this before. In college, I had felt myself beginning to fall for Lauren, to care for her, but it was nothing like this. This was much deeper, stronger. I wanted to tell her I loved her, and I thought about how I should do it.

Then, my phone rang.

"Don't answer it," Lauren dared me.

But I did.

It was Uncle Albert, informing me that my mother had been rushed to hospital after she collapsed at home. The housekeeper found her, apparently. A possible heart attack. I heard the news and felt detached from it somehow.

"Thank you for informing me," I said, rather formally, realizing we'd have to leave. Even here, my mother had managed to reach me and tried to destroy my happiness.

As soon as I told Lauren what had happened, she got up and packed our things. She wanted to leave right away but I insisted that we have breakfast first.

"You need your strength," I said.

But my reasons were entirely selfish. I wasn't ready to leave our forest den, our little hideaway among the trees. It had been fantastic, these past two days with Lauren, all alone, rekindling our relationship and finding that our bond was stronger than it had ever been.

"We have to get to the airport," Lauren said, anxiously looking at her phone.

"She's stable and in hospital," I said. "We'll get there soon enough."

I couldn't tell Lauren about my suspicions, awful as they were. But I couldn't discount completely that my mother had somehow orchestrated this medical emergency to get me back to the city and to the company. She must have realized that I could not be separated from

Lauren and had to find a way to force my hand, bring me back to the city.

But I wanted to hold on to the romance that Lauren and I had found in Colorado. As she walked ahead of me towards the door, I caught her hand and made her stop. She turned to look at me, a question in her eyes.

"I love you, Lauren," I said quietly. "Whatever happens in New York, whatever happened in the past, I want you to know that I love you."

"Oh, Matthew," she flew into my arms, kissing me. "I love you too."

"I want us to be together, like this."

"Me too."

"Let's get our own place in the city. Will you come back to me, live with me at my hotel?"

"Are you seriously not going home?"

I didn't know how to tell her that the cold brick house where I had grown up had never been a home. I'd never felt comfortable there and I was beginning to think that I'd never belonged there to begin with.

"Home is where the heart is," I said and kissed her again, holding her against me for the longest time.

While she went on ahead to the car, I checked my phone for messages.

Then I called the hospital and asked for the doctor who was treating my mother.

I waited while they called him to the phone.

"Dr. Horowitz? This is Matthew Waterstone."

"Ah, yes, Mr. Waterstone. Your mother is resting and comfortable."

"What happened to her? Did she have a heart attack?"

"We ran a few tests, and I am confident we can rule that out. She appears to be dehydrated and anemic and that may have caused her to faint. I am waiting for more results, and we'll keep her overnight, but she will be able to go home tomorrow."

Perhaps I should have felt happiness at hearing of my mother's good health.

But all I felt was anger. I was sure she'd fainted on purpose in a desperate bid to get my attention. I didn't want to tell Lauren what the doctor had said. I felt too much anger towards my mother. There was frustration too, with the fact that she had ruled my entire life and had one way or another, always found a way to get me to do her bidding.

But not this time.

It was time I started living my life, for me.

That would start right now.

Chapter 23

Lauren

"Tell me everything!" my mother demanded that evening.

I was waiting for her at home, with a takeaway curry from our favorite Indian restaurant. I had ordered extra poppadums and mango chutney as well as naan bread. I bought bottles of wine and laid the table, waiting for her to come from work. I hadn't told her I was coming and when she saw me in the kitchen, she squealed with delight and came to hug me straight away.

"I was wondering when you'd be back!" she beamed at me.

"So, how was Colorado?" she asked, helping herself to a glass of wine and sitting down at the table to nibble on a piece of naan.

We had not really talked about my father or me meeting my half-siblings. I didn't want to talk about them while they were around, and during the day my mother was at work. I had known she would expect a full report, and I'd been thinking about what to say to her.

But then everything had happened with Matthew and thoughts of my father had taken a backseat. My mind was filled by the incredible romance of the last couple of days, our secluded getaway at the forest lodge, where we'd finally found each other, and he had told me he loved me. Everything else seemed to pale into insignificance for me, but for my mother, I knew I had to talk about my father first.

"I can see why you fell for him," I said.

"Oh?"

"He's charming, funny and a great guy."

"What does he look like now?"

I showed her some pictures on my mobile.

"Oh, my God, he's so old!" she cried out and I had to scold her.

"He's still good-looking, though!"

"I don't know," she said and pulled a face.

I told her how he'd made me feel welcome, fetching me at the airport and preparing the guest room for me with fresh flowers. I described the meal he, Vern and Ava had cooked for me and how well I'd gotten along with them. She was especially interested to hear about his wife and their divorce, about his various infidelities. When I confronted her about him calling her after she got pregnant, she became thoughtful, playing with a strand of her hair.

"Why didn't you tell me he tried calling you?"

She shrugged. "I didn't know why he wanted to talk to me. I thought maybe he wanted to hook up again. I didn't know he wanted to talk about the pregnancy."

That made sense.

"He could have tried harder, you know, come round to see me? But he'd left it at that."

She was right.

"He had a bit of reputation, even back then. I always knew that he wasn't relationship material. When I got pregnant, I knew from the start that whatever decision I made, I would have to make by myself. My immediate thought was of my own baby and how lucky I was that this was not my situation at all.

"He wants to be a part of the baby's life, as a grandfather," I said, watching expressions change on my mother's face. I could see that it wouldn't be easy for her to have John being a part of my life. She didn't like him being back in my life.

"Would you rather I didn't see him?" I asked.

"No, no, that wouldn't be fair." But she didn't like it.

"Life isn't about fair," I said.

"Hey, that's my line," she said, smiling at me.

I took a sip of wine.

"I have more news," I said, taking a deep breath and telling her about what happened with me and Matthew.

She listened to the whole story and when I told her how he'd said he wanted me to move in together, she drummed her hands on the table and whooped out loud.

"That's wonderful, honey!"

"I know. I am so happy."

She smiled at me, pleased for me, but I saw reservation too.

"Where is he now?"

I told her he was at the hospital visiting his mother. I didn't tell her how quiet he had been on the drive back or on the flight home. He'd barely spoken to me, his faced closed off and shuttered. I could tell he was in some kind of turmoil and reached for his hand. He clasped it tightly and I knew it wasn't me or our relationship. He was dealing with his mother and what this hospitalization of hers meant. He had told me what the doctor said, about how his mother wasn't ill and speculated that she might have had a panic attack. Even though he didn't say it out loud, I sensed he thought she was faking it. Trying to guilt him into coming to see her. It was a terrible thought and I felt deeply sorry for him to have to deal with that. My relationship with my mother was so precious to me, I could not imagine a life in which she was my greatest adversary, or even worse, an enemy.

"Are you sure about him?" she asked, carefully.

"What do you mean?"

"He hurt you so badly in college. Remember how cut up you were? When you started working at the company, you told me what he'd said to you."

"I know." It wasn't easy to talk about this, but I knew it was important. Even if my heart was filled with love and the memory of what had happened between us, I had to be able to talk about our past.

"He's different now."

"I'm worried that you think that now, and then two years down the line, he changes right back. You know a leopard doesn't change its spots?"

"The thing is, he didn't mean the things he'd said to me back then," I said. "He wanted to hurt me because he thought I'd cheated on him. I hadn't, but I can see why he thought that."

I told her about Gabe, and how I'd flirted with him to make his boyfriend jealous.

My mother shook her head. "No wonder he got jealous, that would make any man furious!"

"I guess."

I told her what I had learnt about his family and his mother, about his loneliness growing up and how he'd had to protect himself, by not getting involved with anyone.

"It's like he's never shown his emotions, so, they're all fragile and tender, like new grass shoots," I joked.

"I mean, when I look at myself, the boyfriends I had in high school, the friends I have had and the way we've always been able to talk, it feels like my emotions are stronger, tougher, you know?"

"You're like me, I guess," my mother grinned at me. "We've had to be tough, learn how to roll with the punches.

"Matthew hasn't had that," I said thoughtfully. "He's never allowed himself to feel anything. Even his father's death. He just buried his grief and pretended everything was fine. It turned into anger, I think, and resentment."

"Not healthy."

"No," I thought about it. "That anger has driven him in his life, I think, in his career too. When he became the CEO and took over the company, and he wanted to make it this success. It was the anger at his mother and his fate, I guess, that made him push so hard."

"And take it out on you when you started there."

I nodded. "But once he realized that I was pregnant with his child, it was like he stopped fighting me, stopped trying to beat me, or something."

"Amazing," my mom smiled softly at me. "Love conquers all."

I pulled a face. "I don't know."

I told her about his mother, and how her illness had cast a shadow over everything. "He wants to stand up to her but that may mean an end to their relationship, and he is all she has. His family and the Waterstone legacy are his entire life. Even if he says he doesn't care about it, I think he can't help being affected by all of it."

We sat in silence for a while. My mother poured herself another glass of wine and we lit some candles. The mood was warm, companionable.

"How are things with Vic?" I asked. I think she blushed, but it was hard to tell in the candlelight. She certainly seemed embarrassed.

"Good," she said. Then she laughed and amended, "Very good. I met his son the other night and he introduced me as his girlfriend."

"But that's great!"

My mom laughed, embarrassed. "Oh, I'm too old to be a girlfriend, don't you think?!"

Still, I could tell she was pleased. Perhaps she would be able to make this relationship work after all. I didn't want her to be alone.

"I'm going to go back to the hotel room," I told her.

"You're leaving?" she asked.

"I want to be there when Matthew gets back from the hospital."

She nodded but looked a bit forlorn.

"I can wait a while if you want? I don't think he'll be back yet?"

"No, no, you go," she said, sitting up straighter in her chair.

As I hugged her goodbye, I held her a little while longer, smelling the familiar scent of her shampoo and the perfume she had used for years. I closed my eyes and wondered how Matthew would be when he came back that night. If he would be as tense and withdrawn as he'd been all day. His family had come between us before, and I hoped our love was strong enough to deal with this.

But I wasn't sure.

Chapter 24

Matthew

From the hospital, I went back to the house.

The housekeeper, Rosario, opened the door, anxiously scanning my face for news.

"How is she? How is Mrs. Waterstone?"

"The doctors say she is going to be fine," I reassured her. I told her what the doctor said.

"She's asked for a few things to be brought to her, I said I'd drop it off." I wasn't keen to go through my mother's private things. "Could you pack a bag for her? Some night clothes, toiletries, you know what she likes?"

"Of course, right away."

Rosario rushed upstairs, eager to help. I thought of how rude my mother always was to her, how quick to point out dusty surfaces or flowers that needed changing. But in her time of need, Rosario was the one who wanted to help her.

I thought of how I'd walked into my mother's private hospital room earlier in the afternoon, and saw her lying there, a small figure in the big hospital bed. Her hair was flat, limp and her face had seemed older, pale. I didn't like to see her like that.

She opened her eyes and cried out my name, stretching a hand towards me.

"Matthew!"

I went closer, rather unwillingly. I took her hand and she grasped it tightly. Too tightly.

"Where were you?"

As if I had disappeared without leaving word for weeks. It had only been a few days.

"I was with Lauren," I said.

I saw her face harden, but she did not let go of my hand.

"I'm glad to see you're well," I said. "The doctor said you must have fainted due to dehydration, anemia and low blood pressure."

My mother made a disparaging sound, indicating how little she thought of him.

"I have been so upset about everything," she said. "I had chest pains before it happened."

"They did an EKG. Your heart is fine," I said, pulling my hand from her grasp. "Perhaps it was a panic attack."

My mother made a disparaging noise.

"Do you need anything?"

"I need my son back," my mother said, her voice shaking.

"I'm here," I said.

Then I said, "But I might as well tell you, I've decided to resign as CEO from Egal."

"What?" she cried out and her heart rate monitor started bleeping.

I had thought that of all the places in the world where I could break the news to my mother, a hospital was probably best.

"These last couple of days, being away from the company have been so liberating. I have felt so happy."

"But what about the company?"

"Another family member can take over, Will perhaps?"

"But it was your father's dream that you take over from him!" Tears were running down her face.

"I don't know, Mother. I've started thinking it was more your dream than his. And now that Lauren and I have managed to work things out, I can tell you that my dreams have changed."

She stared at me, too shocked to respond.

"I've been CEO for five years now and I think that is enough."

"But... the future..." Her heart rate went up even more and a nurse came in to check on it. She looked angrily at me, "You need to leave. You're upsetting Mrs. Waterstone."

"No, no!" My mother cried out. "Don't leave. Please, let him stay."

"Five minutes more," the nurse said sternly.

I waited until the nurse was out of the room.

I kept my voice calm, reasonable.

"I have given it a lot of thought. I don't want to upset you, but my future is with Lauren and my baby. Your grandchild. You don't think Father would have wanted me to be in my child's life, the way he could not? You don't think he'd want me to be happy?"

She stared at me, wide-eyed, unable to respond.

"I've made up my mind and you have a choice. You can be in our lives or not. It's up to you, but you will have to apologize to Lauren for that stunt you pulled. I'll go back and get a few things for you."

Perhaps I had been too harsh with my mother, I thought as I left, but I felt I had to get the message across. I had to do it now, while I still could.

In the car on the way to the house, I thought about Lauren and the last couple of days in Colorado. I knew that I wanted to ask her to marry me. I wanted to spend the rest of my life with her, and our child. Lauren made me happy in the way that nobody ever had, in the way no spreadsheet or profit margin had been able to do. The thought of our baby, growing inside of her, gave me such joy as I hardly knew how to express.

Earlier, I had trailed after Rosario, who had gone into my mother's private rooms. I looked at her sitting room with its antique table where I had seen my mother write in her diary and do her accounting. I noticed a television set and some books on the table. It made me uncomfortable to be in this space, and I was loathing going into her bedroom. My mother and I had never been close, despite my father's death. One might have thought that his death would have brought us together and I think that was what I wanted at the time. But my father was the warm, jovial one. She was quieter and more controlling. I looked at the obsessively tidy bedroom and wondered if perhaps her neurosis had gotten the better of her. I had craved attention from her and in the absence of love, I had to do with her approval. The only way to get it, was to do as she'd told me. It was a conditional love and she had used it to control me.

I could see this now.

I also realized that I no longer needed it.

From the safe at the house, I removed my grandmother Alice's engagement ring. After she died, my mother told me that it was mine to give to the woman I was to marry. It was a rather old-fashioned diamond ring, bought by my grandfather before he became the wealthy investor. She had treasured this ring, my mother said, because it had reminded her of their love before the wealth, my grandfather's drinking, and his pomposity.

I was going to propose to Lauren tonight as soon as I'd made a last quick stop at the hospital. I didn't even intend seeing my mother. I would give the nurses the bag with her things and leave for the hotel.

When I got to the hospital, however, the nurse I'd seen earlier came over to me and pulled me aside. She said my mother had been very upset after I left and that they had given her something to help her sleep. "She kept saying how it wasn't supposed to be this way. When I asked her what she meant, she became quite distressed."

I didn't know what to say.

"She loves you very much," the nurse said, touching my arm and squeezing it. "But she doesn't know how to show it."

She looked me in the eye, and I had to look away.

I didn't know what to say to that.

She was right, of course. We had never been comfortable with emotion in our family. My mother thought it was a sign of bad breeding to show too much emotion. She preferred sarcasm and irony to get her point across. I couldn't recall her ever hugging me as a child. She never tucked me in or kissed me goodnight. There was always a nanny to do that. I also had a problem with my emotions, showing anyone what I felt. It was only with Lauren that I felt I could truly be myself and share my thoughts. Since meeting Lauren and being more open with her, I'd found the courage to be more honest in other parts of my life as well. Admitting to how much I hated working at Egal, for instance, and seeing that I wanted to leave the company.

I handed my mother's bag to the nurse, and she told me she'd see to it that my mother would get it.

"We'll keep a close eye on her tonight," She promised me.

I drove to the hotel thinking about what the nurse said. I realized that she was probably right and that however, twisted, and strange, my mother did love me. I loved her too, but that didn't mean I had to allow her to dictate to me how I should lead my life. She had a choice now and while I hoped she made the right one, a part of me was willing to accept that maybe she would not. Perhaps she would choose anger and bitterness over me. The important thing was that I would not. I would no longer carry the anger and resentment of my childhood and upbringing with me. I was ready to let it go.

I couldn't wait to see Lauren at the hotel.

She had told me she was going to see her mother and I thought of the conversation they'd have. Her mother might try to discourage her from coming to stay with me at the hotel. I arrived at the hotel and took the elevator up to my suite near the top. I had given Lauren my key card and had to ask for another one at reception.

When I opened the door to my room, I looked around and saw it was empty.

No Lauren.

I felt my heart sink.

I thought she would be here.

I'd wanted her to be here so badly.

Then the bathroom door opened, and Lauren came out.

"Matthew! I didn't hear you come in."

I took her in my arms and held her against me. My heart was thudding in my chest. The thought that she might not have been here had been terrifying.

"I want us to be together, now and forever," I said. "Will you marry me, Lauren? Be my wife?"

She looked at me, stunned. But then her face lit up as she said, "Yes, of course!" and we kissed for what felt like an eternity.

When we broke apart, she wanted to know how it had gone at the hospital.

"Not now," I said. "My mother is fine; I'll tell you about it later. Right now, I want to see if you will try this on for me."

I took my grandmother's ring from my pocket and slipped it on Lauren's ring finger.

It slid onto her finger without any difficulty.

"We can have it refitted," I said. "You don't have to wear it if you don't like it."

"It's perfect," Lauren said. "I love it." Her eyes shone brighter than any diamond as she looked into my eyes, and for the first time in my life, I knew what it felt like to have everything in life that I needed. All the money, the clothes, eating in the finest restaurants and driving the fastest cars, could not give me this feeling that I had when I held Lauren in my arms. It was as if nothing else mattered. I had a sense of belonging. It had nothing to do with a property or a building or a job, instead it was a different kind of wealth and at the same time, the greatest fortune I could ever have wished for.

Epilogue

Lauren

When I told Ava we were getting married, she immediately asked, "What's the rush? Shouldn't you wait until after the baby's born? At least it won't be almost winter then? And you'll have lost the baby fat."

But I was becoming heavier by the day, bigger and rounder and I didn't want to get married with a baby on my hip.

"We don't want to wait," I said.

"It takes forever to plan a wedding," Ava warned, but I told her that neither of us wanted a big affair.

Matthew was keen to elope, for it to be only the two of us. But I wanted my mother to be there, as well as John, as I'd come to think of my father. There were my friends too and while I understood Matthew's issues with his family, I wondered if he would not regret it later if he did not invite them to his wedding. His mother had come to see me after her release from the hospital, she was rather diminished in size and pride. She apologized for having offered me money to disappear and cried rather unexpectedly when she told me she had never felt such pain as when she thought she'd lost Matthew.

"You will see when you have your child," she whispered to me. "Nothing else matters."

When we told her about the wedding, she offered her father's house, a stately mansion on Long Island. It was an ideal wedding venue, with romantic ivy growing along the front and extensive formal gardens that would be lovely as wedding picture backdrops. The house stood empty since Matthew's grandfather had taken up residency in a nursing home. There were several rooms that I could offer to guests, and it did not take me long to agree to the location on the condition that she let me organize the wedding. I didn't want a fancy society affair. Instead, I appointed my mother as wedding planner and of course, the plans were disorganized. A mix-up with the chairs meant they were not delivered a day before as they should have been. Vic ended up hiring a van and bringing the chairs himself. When my mother checked on the flowers, she realized the deposit had never been paid and the roses had not been ordered. Then two pigeons got into the main dining area, ripping the ornamental organza that had been draped over the windows.

Every time a new problem presented itself, Matthew shook his head and mumbled again about wedding venues in the Bahamas. I loved the old house though, with its ornate façade and the gardens, which we'd fixed up for the wedding. Matthew had presented me with an exquisite Vera Wang wedding gown, a strapless dress with a high waist, and magnificent silk organza skirt. It was simple but elegant, with delicate embroidery on the bodice. I didn't even look pregnant when I had it on and I absolutely loved it.

The day of the wedding was unexpectedly pleasant with a few hours of golden sunshine in the middle of the day, which meant we could have the ceremony outdoors. My mother and Ava scrambled to find a wedding bower of flowers to put up in the garden and chairs were carried outside for the guests. Despite all the last-minute preparations, everything looked perfect. It was a fairytale wedding and everything I could ever have dreamed of.

John came all the way from Colorado with Ava and Vern. He met me in the house to walk me out.

"You look…," he said, choking up, unable to say the words.

My mother came to check on me and when she saw me, took my hands, and kissed them.

"Oh, sweetheart, you look so beautiful."

I smiled at her and saw her and John nod to each other rather stiffly.

But it was time to get married.

I took John's arm and he led me out and down the stone steps to where Matthew was waiting for me. Our guests were sitting on either side of the petal-strewn path and even though everyone was smiling at me, I registered only Matthew's face.

I didn't care about the food or the music, about who managed to make it to the wedding or who didn't. Matthew's Uncle Albert and his sons were there, and he seemed quite emotional after the ceremony, hugging Matthew for a long time afterwards to congratulate him. It turned out that the board did not accept Matthew's resignation and for a few weeks, the negotiations for his return to work affected everyone, causing much tension. But I convinced Matthew to go back, even if it was only for a few months. He agreed eventually, but only for a short while and to prepare Will to take over for him.

After the ceremony, we went inside for the reception.

There were a number of speeches, but I remembered my mother's best of all. She looked lovely in a flowery dress that showed off her slim figure. Her hair had been cut and lightened for the occasion and Vic had only eyes for her, which was as it should be.

"Lauren and I always had a Chinese restaurant that we liked to go to," my mother's speech began. "Sometimes we got take aways, and other times we would sit down for our favorite dishes. When she was smaller, it was kung pao chicken, but later, of course, it had to be vegetarian."

The audience laughed and my mother went on.

"One time, she was probably around twelve years old, I went to pay the bill. They usually had fortune cookies at the till and Lauren loved these. They didn't have any that day, Lauren was so disappointed. But the old Chinese lady behind the till said to me in a heavy accent, not to worry. She pointed at Lauren and winked at me, saying 'she lucky, she needs no cookie.'"

Everyone laughed again. I didn't remember this story at all.

My mother smiled. "I would never forget that. I also never told anyone the story because I didn't want to jinx it! There were so many times when things could have gone wrong, but they didn't. When I forgot to fetch her from school once and another parent kindly took her home. Or when the school bus had an accident on the way to a class outing and Lauren happened not to go that day. I always felt something, or someone was protecting her. Then later, when she came back from college and struggled to find work, I knew she would find something eventually, and she did. And I also realized, Lauren makes her own luck. She doesn't wait around for good things to happen, she makes them happen. Stick around with this one, Matthew and good things will happen to you too."

She raised her glass, and everyone drank a toast to us.

Tears were running down my cheeks and I went up to hug her.

"Where did all that come from?" I asked her, laughing through my tears.

I knew my mother didn't like public speaking, yet she had managed that story perfectly.

"I've been practicing," she said, crying too.

"I can vouch for that," Vic said, his eyes twinkling.

It was a magical day that I knew I would never forget.

There wasn't much time for a honeymoon, but Matthew insisted we go back to the resort in Colorado where we had spent those magical few days and realized we were in love. Shortly after that, I went into the last part of the pregnancy, becoming heavy and super uncomfortable. I had trouble sleeping at night and Matthew made finding our own place a priority. Cynthia wanted us to move in with her, but Matthew was firm. We hired a rental property on a week-by-week basis while looking at properties.

I understood that he wanted a fresh start for us as a family, but I felt sorry for his mother. She had aged visibly since her heart scare. Matthew's relationship with her was cordial but strained. She was trying her best to repair the rift between them, but she had never been an emotional woman and Matthew could be very stubborn.

In the end, it was the baby that brought them together.

Jonathan Egbert Waterstone was born a week early, in the middle of a cold winter's night. Matthew and I had gone to dinner even though

I'd barely been able to eat anything, feeling so bloated and big. But Matthew thought going out would take my mind off the baby and halfway through the main course, my water broke. I couldn't believe it, it was so embarrassing, but Matthew calmly went to get my coat and quietly helped me out of the restaurant without anyone noticing.

We went straight to the hospital, only to be told that the baby was not yet due. I was in labor, but it could take hours. After months of waiting, the baby was finally coming and both of us were petrified. What if something went wrong? Matthew went a deathly pale and paced up and down the hospital corridors while I screamed for pain killers.

In the end, our baby came quickly.

He weighed a healthy seven pounds and after ten hours of labor, I was exhausted. Matthew was with me for the whole ordeal, holding my hand and staying by my side.

When they put my son, bundled up in fuzzy blankets in my arms afterwards, I couldn't believe that the pain and discomfort had produced this tiny little human, with perfect hands and feet. When Cynthia Waterstone came to see her grandson the following day, she immediately exclaimed,

"You looked just like that after you were born! With a full head of hair! Just like him!"

Matthew handed her the baby and she at first shook her head.

"No, no, I don't want to drop him."

But Matthew was firm. "Just hold him, like this," he said, pushing the baby gently into her arms. She stood stiffly, holding the baby and I watched her face change as she held him, properly looking at him.

"I wish your father could have been here to see this," she whispered. "He would have been so proud of the man you've become."

Later, when Matthew went with the nurse and our son for a doctor's visit, Cynthia awkwardly came to my bedside.

"I'm sorry," she said. "About everything."

She'd apologized before but this time, I knew she meant it.

"Any fool can see that boy is a Waterstone. That nose and the chin... I mean, obviously."

The previous day, my mother had said the baby reminded her of me as a baby. It was hilarious, but in a way, also touching to see how a baby brought the family together.

No-one could be prouder than Matthew.

He refused to go home, staying with me and Jonny, as I was beginning to think of him. He sat in the easy chair they had brought into the room for him, rocking the baby back and forth, singing old rock ballads to him.

"Don't you know any lullabies?" I teased him.

"Nothing wrong with the classics," he said, as he sang another verse of Hotel California to the sleeping baby.

Our new house was outside of the city, a Georgian brick house with a huge stretch of lawn and trees. We'd looked at so many houses by then, but when we saw this place, both of us could see us living there. There were two storeys, and vast rooms, more than I knew what we could do with.

"It's so quiet here," I said, marveling at the lack of city noises. "But isn't it too far from the city?"

"Yeah, but I don't have to go to the office every day now. And there is plenty of space for the kids to cycle and play," said Matthew, peering down the wide, tree-lined avenues.

"What kids?" I asked him, with a smile.

He didn't say anything then, but later as we drove back, he told me of a dream he'd had. He wanted to talk to me about it, to see what I thought. I could see he was a bit nervous about the idea. Then he said, "I've been thinking," he said. "About us fostering a child. Maybe two, but one to begin with."

"A foster child?"

The last couple of months, Matthew had been undergoing so many changes. It started when he made peace with his mother one evening. She came over for dinner and we had a bottle of wine. I went to bathe Jonathan and I heard them talking downstairs. I came down and saw that Matthew had opened another bottle of wine. Cynthia was talking about Bert and some Christmas when she gave the cook the day off and tried to make roast lamb and forgot all about the meat in the oven, ruining it completely.

"I remember that!" Matthew exclaimed. "We had frozen pizza with the roast potatoes and salad! It was one of the best Christmas lunches ever!"

"It was a nightmare!" Cynthia said. "I was furious with myself, but your father just laughed and heated more pizza!" She closed her eyes. "Your father was always more forgiving than I was." Cynthia said in a brittle voice. "But I think I became even less forgiving after he died." She paused. "For a long time, I couldn't even forgive him for dying."

Things were different between them after that evening.

After quitting Egal, Matthew started working with a children's charity in the city. He told me he was thinking a lot about children who didn't have the opportunities that he'd had in his life. He wanted to help others. He'd met a boy there and he wanted to become a foster parent.

"I know it's a big move," he said. "I don't know how you feel about it."

I had my hands full with the baby and was feeling so overwhelmed by motherhood. Every day, something new seemed to crop up; an allergy I hadn't known about or a rash that looked nasty. I didn't know if I had it in me to take on other people's children and their problems.

"I was thinking, what if we started only with weekends? I could take him fishing, the way my granddad did with me?"

I could handle that.

The following weekend, Matthew came home with Trevor, a quiet 16-year-old with terrible skin and a bad attitude. Over the next few months, Trevor slowly started warming to us and I guess I got used to him. It became a thing, Matthew would take Trevor golfing or hiking, and my mother would come over to watch Jonathan while I did some shopping. On Sundays, we had a big meal as a family and sometimes my mother and Vic joined us. Matthew would talk about the stock market casually, almost as if he was thinking aloud. I knew he was trying to share some of his knowledge with Trevor, possibly interest him in the financial markets. He'd already told me how smart Trevor was and that he intended to pay for his studies if he chose to go to college.

One morning, I woke up to find his side of the bed empty.

I went looking for him in our house, half-asleep, stumbling through the big rooms I was still getting used to. I found him on the couch in our living room, the baby in his arms, both fast asleep. The place was covered in blankets and pillows that he'd turned to face the couch to ensure Jonathan didn't fall off. I leaned forward to adjust the hood away from the baby's face and Matthew's eyes fluttered open.

"Hey, beautiful," he said to me with a tired smile.

I looked at his two-day stubble, the hair that had grown too long and was hanging in his eyes. He was a far cry from the jet-setting businessman he'd been only a year ago when I started working at the company. But there was something incredibly sexy about this Matthew, who had happily traded in his sports car for a less fancy model that could accommodate baby seats and a stroller in the boot. This Matthew no longer had six pack and rock-hard abs, but his eyes were softer, and he smiled more. He was kinder, he was more loving and maybe as a result, he was happier.

I was happier too.

He may have broken my heart once, but he had mended it too.

I was the one who gave him a second chance, but he had given me more happiness than I'd ever known and a meaning to life that I didn't even know existed. I had no idea what the future held for us, but I was no longer afraid, no longer worried about it. I knew we could handle it, together.

*****

Don't miss out!

Visit the website below and you can sign up to receive emails whenever Erica Frost publishes a new book. There's no charge and no obligation.

https://books2read.com/r/B-A-YRSV-OMJKC

Also by Erica Frost

Seduced By A Billionaire
Dark Secrets
A Billionaire's Game
Power Play
Ruthless Rival
Taming The Billionaire
The Hated Billionaire
3-Pointer
Baby For The Billionaire

9 798223 279068